ETGAR KERET

Missing Kissinger

VINTAGE BOOKS
London

Published by Vintage 2008

13

First published as *Ga-aguai Le-Kissinger*, by Zmora Bitan, Tel Aviv 1994

All the stories are new translations except for those marked with astericks. *first published in *The Story about the Bus Driver*, St Martins, New York, 2001. **first published in *Gaza Blues*, David Paul, London, 2004. ***first published in *One Last Story and That's It*, Katha, New Delhi, 2005.

Stories translated by Miriam Shlesinger: *Breaking the Pig, So Good, Missing Kissinger, The Hollow Men*** , A No-Magician Birthday, Hat Trick, Hole in the Wall* , Sidewalks*** , World Champion*** , Painting, My Brother's Depressed, The Sad Story of the Anteater Family, The Monkey's Uncle, Cocked and Locked* , Korbi's Girl, Good Intentions* , Clean Shave*** , Bubbles, Dinosaur Eggs, Hope They Die, Raising the Bar, The Real Winner of the Preliminary Games, A Foreign Language, Drops, Shoes, My Best Friend*

Stories translated by Sondra Silverston: *The Stuff Dreams are Made Of, Cramps, King of the Barbers, Refrigerator, Atonement, Gaza Blues, An Exclusive, Magicians School, Ants, Freeze, Another Option, Without Her, Buffalo, Patience, The Summer of '76*

First published in Great Britain in 2007 by
Chatto and Windus
Random House, 20 Vauxhall Bridge Road,
London SW1V 2SA

www.vintage-books.co.uk

Addresses for companies within The Random House Group Limited can be found at: www.randomhouse.co.uk/offices.htm

The Random House Group Limited Reg. No. 954009

A CIP catalogue record for this book is available from the British Library

ISBN 9780099498162

MIX
Paper from
responsible sources
FSC® C018179

Printed and bound in Great Britain by Clays Ltd, St Ives plc

To Uzi and to my brother

CONTENTS

BREAKING THE PIG

Dad wouldn't buy me a Bart Simpson doll. Mom really wanted to, but Dad wouldn't, he said I was spoilt.

'Why should we?' he said to Mom. 'Why should we buy it for him? He just snaps his fingers and you jump to attention.' Dad said I had no respect for money and that if I didn't learn when I was little when was I going to learn? Kids who get Bart Simpson dolls at the drop of a hat turn into punks who steal from convenience stores, 'cos they wind up thinking they can have whatever they want, just like that. So instead of a Bart doll he bought me an ugly porcelain pig with a slot in its back, and now I'll grow up to be okay, now I won't turn into a punk.

Every morning, now, I'm supposed to drink a cup of hot cocoa, even though I hate it. With the skin it's one shekel, without the skin it's half a shekel, and if I throw up right after I drink it, I don't get anything. I drop the coins into the slot in the pig's back, and then, when you shake him you can hear them jingle. Soon as the pig is so full of coins that it doesn't jingle when you shake it, I get a Bart-Simpson-on-a-skateboard doll. That's what Dad says, that way it's educational.

The pig is kind of cute actually, his nose is cool when you touch it, and he smiles when you drop a shekel in his back, and even when you only drop in half a shekel. But the nicest thing is how he smiles even when you don't. I made up a name for him, too. I call him Margolis, same as the man who used to live in our mailbox and my dad couldn't get the sticker off. Margolis isn't like my other toys. He's much more easygoing, without bulbs or springs or batteries that leak inside. You just have to make sure he doesn't jump off the table.

'Margolis, be careful! You're made of porcelain,' I remind him when I spot him bending over a little and looking down at the floor, and he smiles at me and waits patiently for me to take him down myself. I really love it when he smiles, and I drink the hot cocoa with the skin every morning just for him, so I can drop the shekel in his back and watch how his smile doesn't change at all.

'I love you, Margolis,' I tell him then. 'Honest, I love you more than Mom and Dad. And I'll always love you, no matter what, even if you become a punk. But don't you dare go jumping off the table!'

Yesterday, Dad came in, picked Margolis up off the table and started shaking him upside down real hard.

'Be careful, Dad,' I told him. 'You're giving Margolis a tummy ache.' But Dad didn't stop.

'It isn't making any noise. You know what that means, don't you, Davie? That tomorrow you're going to get that Bart-Simpson-on-a-skateboard doll.'

'Great, Dad,' I said. 'A Bart-Simpson-on-a-skate-board doll, that's great. Just please stop shaking Margolis, before he starts feeling sick.' Dad put Margolis down and went to get Mom. He came back a minute later, pulling Mom behind him with one hand and holding a hammer in the other.

'You see, I was right,' he said to Mom. 'This way he'll know how to appreciate things, won't you, Davie?'

'Sure I will,' I said. 'Sure I will, but what's the hammer for?'

'It's for you,' Dad said and put the hammer in my hand. 'Just be careful.'

'Sure, I'll be careful,' I said, and I really was. But a few minutes later, Dad lost his patience and he said, 'So come on. Break the pig already.'

'What?' I asked. 'Break Margolis?'

'Yes, yes. Margolis,' Dad said. 'Come on, break it. You earned your Bart Simpson, you worked hard enough for it.'

Margolis gave me the sad smile of a porcelain pig who knows his end is near. The hell with Bart Simpson. Me – hit a friend on the head with a hammer?

'I don't want Simpson,' I said and handed the hammer back to Dad. 'Margolis is good enough for me.'

'You don't get it,' Dad said. 'It's really all right, it's educational. Come on, let me break it for you.' Dad raised the hammer and I caught the tired look in Mom's eyes and the broken smile on Margolis's face, and knew it was all up to me now. Unless I did something, he was dead.

'Dad,' I said, grabbing him by the leg.

'What is it, Davie?' Dad said, still holding the hammer high in the air. 'Could I have one more shekel please?' I begged. 'Please give me one more shekel to drop into Margolis, tomorrow, after my hot cocoa. Then I'll break him, tomorrow, I promise.'

'One more shekel?' Dad smiled and put the

hammer down on the table. 'You see? The boy has developed an awareness.'

'Yes, an awareness,' I said. 'Tomorrow.' There were tears in my throat.

Soon as they left the room, I gave Margolis an extra-tight hug and let the tears pour out. Margolis didn't say a thing, he just trembled quietly in my hands. 'Don't worry,' I whispered in his ear. 'I'll save you.'

That night I waited for Dad to finish watching TV in the living room and go to bed. Then I got up very very quietly and sneaked out through the balcony, with Margolis. We walked together in the dark for a very long time till we reached a field of thornbushes.

'Pigs love fields,' I told Margolis as I put him down on the floor of the field, 'especially fields with thornbushes. You'll like it here.' I waited for his answer, but Margolis didn't say a thing, and when I touched him on the nose to say goodbye he just gave me a sad look. He knew he'd never see me again.

SO GOOD

Wearing nothing but pajama bottoms and cowboy boots, Itzik sat on the edge of the bed and stared out of the window. The sun was shining out there. He felt like a jerk. Happiness was supposed to arrive today. His sources had just informed him about it five minutes ago, and here he was, sitting on the bed like an idiot, not doing a thing about it. He thought back over the last time Happiness had come – how his father had opened the door for it, just like that, and how Itzik himself, a pale-faced little boy, had just sat there at the kitchen table making paper collages, not afraid of anything.

He started trembling. 'It mustn't get in,' he whispered. 'No matter what.' If only he could keep it from getting inside, everything would be okay. He lunged towards the dresser, and started pushing it towards the door. After blocking the entrance completely, he got out his hunting rifle and started shoving the cartridges into it. This time, he'd be ready. Not like at his parents' house. Nobody's going to turn him into a grinning zombie who loves TV soaps and Márquez, and kisses his mother every chance he gets. 'Where's my flak jacket?' he yelled to himself. 'Where's my flak jacket, son-of-a-bitch?' He rummaged frantically through the cabinet under the sink till he found it, put on an undershirt, then the jacket. Next he stuck the ice picks and Stanley knives into the fireplace, with the blades pointing straight up. If they're so clever, let them try the chimney. He'd teach them a thing or two about Happiness. Five years at Club Med. Five years, damn them to hell. With the girl he loved, with oral/anal sex, with money to spend like there's no tomorrow. He'd had it real bad. He knew what it felt like. If Grandma hadn't died, he'd still be stuck there.

The first to arrive was Opportunity. They always sent her in first, like some goddamn Bedouin scout. Probably figured she was expendable. She knocked at the door, then tried the handle, which was electrified. The shock stunned her to the ground. That's when Itzik broke the window with the rifle butt and stuck the barrel out. 'Think of something nice,' he muttered through clenched teeth, and pressed the trigger. 'Think of something nice, you bitch, all the way up to Heaven. I'm not giving in without a fight. I'm not my father. I won't let you drag me away in a van festooned with Walt Disney characters, with a moronic smile splashed all over my face.' He pumped another slug into blank-faced Opportunity just to be on the safe side.

Suddenly he remembered what Greenberg had said about the fast one they pulled using cable TV. Son-of-a-bitch. Here he was, sitting around like a dumb-ass rookie, with his back to the Family Channel, like he'd never heard about what HBO did to the Depression Underground in Seattle back in '87. How stupid could he be! He spun around and fired another one into the TV, a split second before Cosby kissed Lisa. 'Gotta stay cool,' he muttered under his breath. 'Gotta stay cool, no matter what happens.'

He was just beginning to focus on Somalia when he heard rustling in the bushes. It was Sheer Enjoyment with the takeaway pizzas and the porn mags, inching her way along the hedge. He couldn't quite get her in his sights. But she didn't try to get any closer.

'Hey, babe, I hate my pizzas cold,' he screamed. But she didn't even answer. The helicopters were overhead now, with their enormous loudspeakers booming techno hits and schmaltzy crooners at top volume. He put his hands over his ears, and concentrated on Holocaust Memorial Day, on women with their breasts cut off, on homeless people shivering in the New York winter. He did have a hint of a smile on his face, but the music remained on the outside. Still, there was something going on. It all seemed too easy. The helicopters. Sheer Enjoyment not making a move. It must be a ploy. 'The roof, damn it,' he blurted. 'It's gotta be the roof.' He took a few pot shots through the shingles. Something fell down the chimney straight onto the spikes. That was Success! She was holding a packet of winning lottery tickets. Itzik doused her with gasoline and threw his Zippo into the fireplace. The body caught fire instantly. Along with the winning tickets. The flames lapped them up long before they had a chance to spread through the cabin. Smoke was filling the room, mixed with another smell, the fragrance of hot corn on the cob, of old-fashioned ice cream, of Mom tucking him in at night. Gas. He crawled along the floor, trying to get to the gas masks. AIDS, he thought to himself. People abusing children all over the world at this very moment. Children. So sweet, I'd love to have some of my own, and a wife. Who loves me. Being tortured in the Secret Service dungeons – he tried. No way. The smile just kept spreading. Threatening to swallow him up. Three emotions he couldn't quite make out were taking over, removing his flak jacket, wiping the number off his arm with saliva. Replacing his '*Why?*' undershirt with a '*Don't Worry, Be Happy*' one. Don't lose hope, it'll work out, he said, trying to cheer himself up as they dragged him out on to the porch. She'll be there, waiting for you. You'll have an amazing future. You'll have an APV Minivan. So intense was the anticipation that his knees were turning to mush. You'll have it so good, son-of-a-bitch, so good.

The tears in his throat had dried up by then. The trees were all green on the outside. And the sky was bright blue. The weather was just right, not too warm and not too cold. A van covered with *Simpsons* characters and mortgage ads was there already, waiting for him at the bottom of the stairs.

MISSING KISSINGER

She says I don't really love her. That I say I do, that I think I do, but that I don't. I've heard of people who say they don't love someone, but to decide for someone else if he loves them? That's a new one to me. Truth is, I had it coming. He who goes to bed with a skunk shouldn't complain that his children stink. She's been bugging me for six months already. Sticking her fingers up her cunt after we fuck to check if I really came, and me, instead of saying something, I tell her, 'It's all right, baby, we're all a little insecure.'

So now she wants us to break up, because she's decided I don't love her. What can I tell her? If I yell at her to stop acting like a jerk and to quit making things up, it'll only prove her point.

'Do something to show that you love me,' she says. What does she want me to do? What? She just has to name it. But she won't. Because if I really loved her I'd figure it out for myself. One thing, though, she's ready either to give me a hint about what it is, or to say what it isn't. One or the other, I get to choose. So I ask her to tell me what it isn't, that way at least we'll know something.

The only sure thing about her clues is that I won't understand them. 'What it isn't,' she says, 'is anything to do with maiming yourself, like poking an eye out or slashing an ear off, because then you'd be hurting someone I love, and indirectly you'd be hurting me too. And hurting someone close is definitely no proof of love.'

Truth is, I'd never have hurt myself even if she hadn't said that. What does poking an eye out have to do with love anyway? And how about telling me what it is? That she won't do, except to say that it wouldn't be a good thing to do to my father or my sisters or brothers either. I'm ready to give up, and tell myself there's no point, nothing is going to help me. Or her. He who plays practical jokes on dodgy crackheads shouldn't cry about broken bones. But later, when we fuck and she stares deep into my eyes – she never closes her eyes when we fuck, so that I won't put someone else's tongue in her mouth – suddenly it hits me, like a revelation. 'Is it my mother?' I ask, but she refuses to answer.

'If you really love me, you'll know for yourself.' And after tasting the fingers she's retrieved from her cunt she blurts out, 'And don't you go bringing me an ear or a finger or anything like that. It's her heart I want, you hear me? Her heart.'

I carry the knife with me all the way to Petah Tikva, on two buses. A knife five feet long, so big it takes up a double seat. I have to buy an extra ticket for it. What won't I do for her? What won't I do for you, Angel Puss? I walk the entire length of Stempfer Street with the knife on my back, like some Arab *shahid*. Mom knew I'd be coming, so she made me a meal, with spices out of hell, like only she knows how to make. I eat without saying a word. He who swallows prickly pears with the spikes on shouldn't gripe about hemorrhoids.

'And how is Miri?' Mom asks. 'Is she okay, the darling girl? Still pushing her chubby fingers up herself?'

'She's okay,' I tell her. 'She's really okay. She asked for your heart. You know, to find out if I love her.'

'Bring her Baruch's,' Mom laughs. 'She'll never know the difference.'

'Come off it, Mom!' I say, angry. 'We're not into lying and stuff. Miri and I are into honesty.'

'All right,' Mom sighs. 'So bring her mine. I don't want you fighting on account of me. Which reminds me, what about your proof to your loving mother that you love her back a little too?'

Furiously, I fling Miri's heart down on the table. Why won't those two believe me? Why are they always testing me? And now I'm going to have to take two buses again, all the way back with this knife, and Mom's heart. And I bet she won't even be home, she'll be back with her old boyfriend. Not that I blame anyone but myself.

There are two kinds of people, those who like to sleep next to the wall and those who like to sleep next to the ones who'll push them out of bed.

THE HOLLOW MEN

When I was a little boy, there used to be all kinds of people coming to our house, knocking on our front door. Dad would look through the peephole but he wouldn't open up. And they'd knock on our door, banging wildly, and I was a little scared of them. But Dad would always come over to me, lie down on the carpet next to me, with his back against the piano, hugging me real tight. 'Don't be scared,' he'd whisper. 'There's nothing to be scared of. It's just the hollow people.' And Dad would whisper in my ear, 'Shiffman, open the door. We know you're in there,' and a second later the people would repeat what Dad had said, but out loud. And then they'd circle the house a few times, trying to open the shutters from the outside, and Dad would mutter in my ear and they would mutter the same thing from the outside, like an echo. 'You see,' Dad would whisper again. 'There's nothing to be scared of. Those people are hollow, with no body, nothing, just voices.' And Dad would whisper, 'We'll be back, Shiffman, you picked on the wrong guy.' And they'd repeat after him. And they'd always come back, the hollow people, and we'd always hide.

And Mom died without a voice, but with a body, and we went to bury her. We brought along a person who would cry over her and Dad showed me in the book exactly what cries because that man was one of them too. Then it was quiet for a week, but after that they came again. We stayed huddled in the corner. Sometimes Dad would say what they would say, and sometimes I did. And inside me I was surprised at how I used to be so scared and now my words bounced off them like a tennis ball thrown against the wall. Quiet and meaningless. And Dad died too in that corner beside the piano, with me giving him the same hug he used to give me back then when I was still scared. He was silent as we lowered him into the grave, and he was silent when the man who does the crying gave the cries that I knew he'd give from the book, and he was silent when we covered him with dirt. And I was silent after him, because when all was said and done, I guess I was one of them too.

A NO-MAGICIAN BIRTHDAY

In November '93, Dov Genichovsky announced the new municipal tax collection ordinance on national radio. My mother, who even at fifty-three was still a dazzling beauty, had begun to drag her feet across the floor. Her smile stayed the same and so did her hugs, and she still had a lot of strength left in her arms, but when she walked her feet wouldn't go all the way up any more. If you looked hard at the X-rays, you could spot black worms drilling into her kidneys. My birthday was coming up. A date that's very easy to remember: 21 December, 21/12. I knew she'd be planning something special, the way she does every year.

The winter of '93 was probably the coldest winter of my life. I was living on my own, sleeping in sweats and socks, and every night, I'd make sure to tuck the top part deep into my pants so if I turned in my sleep, my back would still be covered. The Channel Two project had just fallen through, the paper wouldn't give me a raise, and my ex-girlfriend was going around town telling everyone I was gay and impotent. I'd wake up in the middle of the night with my armpits stinking of decay. I'd call her, and as a precaution I'd put my hand over the receiver even when I was dialing – and when she'd answer I'd hang up. I was convinced I was getting back at her big time.

We put off my birthday by a day, because on the evening of the twentieth the paper sent me to an observatory to bring back a thousand words about a group of meteors that only traveled past us every hundred years. I asked if I could write about the settler from Hebron who'd been hit in the head and turned into a vegetable, but they told me it wasn't my niche. My precise niche was human interest. Every week I was supposed to do the human interest thing for pages 16–17 of the supplement, so that whoever had managed to get through the security-crime-finance-politics stories would get a bonus: a world convention of veterinarians, skateboard championship of the universe, something upbeat. I kept trying for the settler who'd gotten whacked on the head with a brick, I felt a strong bond with him. His project had fallen through, too, and his future wasn't looking too bright. But the editor wouldn't budge, so I headed for the Hadera Observatory with a photographer I'd never met. This photographer told me he'd been pissed off at the paper for the past month or so. He had in his possession the picture of a soldier who'd been murdered in the territories – a blood-and-gore shot of the guy's head skewered on a spike – and the wimpy editor was refusing to print it, said it was cheap.

'I'll bet he'd say that about Lynch, too,' the photographer hissed, taking it out on the gear-stick of our rental car. 'And Peckinpahs are a dime a dozen, too. The picture I shot of that Almakayess guy belongs in a museum, not in a newspaper.'

I tried to guess what my mother would be setting up for my birthday. The present would probably be a mini-cassette recorder. That was the thing I needed most anyway. And she'd bake me a carrot cake just for the occasion, because it's my favorite. We'd sit around and chat, my brother would drive in especially from Ra'ananna. My dad would tell me how proud he was of me, and he'd show me a scrapbook with all the stories I've written pasted on the black pages. I don't know why, but it made me think of my tenth birthday, how the whole class came, and my parents invited a magician.

The photographer and I reached the observatory. It was freezing, and I was supposed to be talking with all the meteor buffs who were hanging around there to get some good quotes for the story. The people I met told me these weren't just meteors that move past us every one hundred years, but a group of meteors that passes by planet earth once in seven centuries. My tape wasn't working, so I had to take everything down in longhand.

'What a bunch of crap this is,' the photographer griped. 'People on the West Bank are slaughtering each other, and here I am shooting short-sighted nerds in anoraks jerking off on a telescope. I hope that at least those stones in the sky come out good.'

Besides the cake, my mother will make the spaghetti I love, and carrot soup. And every time she walks towards the kitchen with those tired steps of hers, I'll want to die.

The meteors arrived the way they do every seven hundred years, and the photographer said it looked like garbage and that in the paper it would look even worse. Considering they only come once in such a long time, he said, the least they could do was give us our money's worth. And I kept thinking that if there was no magician, those meteors should come to our house instead. And that they should burn everything down. My mother, my brother, the worms in her stomach, me, with my thousand words for pages 16–17. Then everyone would be happy, even my ex-girlfriend would sleep easier at night. Like that birthday with the magician, when the coins kept spilling out of my brother's ears and mine. When my mother floated on air like a ballerina on the moon, when my father just smiled and said nothing.

HAT TRICK

At the end of the show, I pull a rabbit out of a hat. I always do it at the end, because kids love animals. At least I did when I was a kid. That way I can end the show on a high note, at the point when I pass the rabbit around so the kids can pet it and feed it. At least, that's how it used to be once. It's harder with today's kids; they don't get as excited. But still, I leave the rabbit for the end. It's the trick I love the most, or rather, it *was* the trick I loved the most. My eyes stay fixed on the audience, as my hand reaches into the hat, groping deep inside it till it feels Kazam's ears.

And then 'Allakazeem – Allakazam!' and out it comes. It never fails to surprise them. And not only them, me too. Every time my hand touches those funny ears inside the hat I feel like a magician. And even though I know how it's done, the hollow space in the table and all that, it still seems like genuine witchcraft.

That Saturday afternoon in the suburbs I left the hat trick to the end like I always do. The kids at that birthday party were incredibly blasé. Some of them had their backs to me, watching a Schwarzenegger movie on cable. The birthday boy wasn't even in the room, he was playing with his new video game. My audience had dwindled to a total of about four kids. It was a particularly stifling day. I was sweating like crazy under my magician's suit. All I wanted was to get it over with and go home. So I skipped over three rope tricks and went straight to the hat. My hand disappeared deep inside it, and my eyes sank into the eyes of a chubby girl with glasses. The soft touch of Kazam's ears took me by surprise the way it always does. 'Allakazeem – Allakazam!' One more minute in the father's den and I'm out of there, with a 300-shekel check in my pocket. I pulled Kazam by the ears, and something about him felt a little strange, lighter. My hand swung up in the air, my eyes still fixed on the audience. And then – suddenly there was this wetness on my wrist and the chubby girl started to scream. In my right hand I was holding

Kazam's head, with his long ears and wide-open rabbit eyes. Just the head, no body. The head, and lots and lots of blood. The chubby girl kept screaming. The kids sitting with their backs to me turned away from the TV and started applauding me. The birthday kid with the new video game came in from the other room, and when he saw the severed head, started whistling enthusiastically. I could feel my lunch rising to my throat. I vomited into my magician's hat, and the vomit disappeared. The kids around me were ecstatic.

That night, I didn't sleep a wink. I checked my gear over and over again. I had no explanation at all for what had happened. Couldn't find the rest of Kazam either. In the morning, I went to the magicians' shop. They were baffled too. I bought a rabbit. The salesman tried to talk me into getting a turtle. 'Rabbits are passé,' he said. 'Turtles are in these days. Tell 'em it's a Ninja turtle and their jaws will drop.'

I bought a rabbit anyway. I named it Kazam too. When I got home, I found five messages on my answering machine. All of them job offers. All of them from kids who'd been at the performance. In one of them, the kid even insisted that I leave the severed head behind just like I'd done at the party. It was only then that I realized I hadn't taken Kazam's head with me.

My next performance was on Wednesday. A ten-year-old in one of the classiest neighborhoods was having a birthday. I was stressed out all through the whole show. Couldn't focus. I slipped up on the trick with the Queen of Hearts. All I could think of was the hat. Finally it was time: 'Allakazeem – Allakazam!' The penetrating look at the audience, the hand into the hat. I couldn't find the ears, but the body was the right weight. Smooth, but the right weight. And then the screaming again. Screaming, but applause too. It wasn't a rabbit I was holding, it was a dead baby.

I can't do that trick any more. I used to love it, but just thinking about it now makes my hands shake. I keep imagining the awful things I'll wind up pulling out of there, the things waiting inside. Last night I dreamt I put my hand into the hat and it was caught in the jaws of a monster. I find it hard to understand how I used to have the courage to push my hand into that dark place. How I used to have the courage to shut my eyes and fall asleep.

I don't perform at all any more, but I don't really care. I don't earn a living, but that's fine too. Sometimes I still put on the suit at home, just for kicks, or I check the secret space in the table under the hat, but that's all. Other than that I keep away from magic tricks, other than that I don't do anything. I just lie awake in bed and think about the rabbit's head and the dead baby. Like they're clues to a riddle, like someone was trying to tell me something, that this isn't the best time for rabbits, or for babies either. That this isn't really the right time for magicians.

HOLE IN THE WALL

On Bernadotte Avenue, right next to the Central Bus Station, there's a hole in the wall. There used to be an ATM there once, but it broke or something, or else nobody ever used it, so the people from the bank came in a pickup and took it, and never brought it back.

Somebody once told Udi that if you scream a wish into this hole, it comes true, but Udi didn't really buy that. The truth is that once, on his way home from the movies, he screamed into the hole in the wall that he wanted Dafne Rimalt to fall in love with him, and nothing happened. And once, when he was feeling really lonely, he screamed into the hole in the wall that he wanted to have an angel for a friend, and an angel really did show up right after that, but he was never much of a friend, and he'd always disappear just when Udi really needed him. This angel was skinny and all stooped and he wore a trench coat the whole time to hide his wings. People in the street were sure he was a hunchback. Sometimes, when it was just the two of them, he'd take the coat off. Once he even let Udi touch the feathers on his wings. But when there was anyone else in the room, he always kept it on. Klein's kids asked him once what he had under his coat, and he said it was a backpack full of books that didn't belong to him and he didn't want them to get wet. Actually, he lied all the time. He told Udi such stories you could die: about places in heaven, about people who when they go to bed at night leave the car keys in the ignition, about cats that aren't afraid of anything and don't even know the meaning of 'scat'. The stories he made up were something else, and to top it all, he'd cross-his-heart-and-hope-to-die.

Udi was nuts about him and always tried hard to believe him. Even lent him some money a couple of times when he was hard up. As for the angel, he didn't do a thing to help Udi. He just talked and talked and talked, rambling on with his hare-brained stories. In the six years he knew him, Udi never saw him so much as rinse a glass.

When Udi was in basic training, and really needed someone to talk to, the angel suddenly disappeared on him for two solid months. Then he came back with an unshaven don't-ask-what-happened face. So Udi didn't ask, and on Saturday they sat around on the roof in their underpants just taking in the sun and feeling low. Udi looked at the other rooftops with the cable hookups and the solar panels and the sky. It occurred to him suddenly that in all their years together he'd never once seen the angel fly.

'How about flying around a little?' he said to the angel. 'It would make you feel better.'

And the angel said: 'Forget it. What if someone sees me?'

'Be a sport,' Udi nagged. 'Just a little. For my sake.' But the angel just made this disgusting noise from the inside of his mouth and shot a gob of spit and white phlegm at the tar-covered roof.

'Never mind.' Udi sulked. 'I bet you don't know how to fly anyway.'

'Sure I do,' the angel shot back. 'I just don't want people to see me, that's all.'

On the roof across the way they saw some kids throwing a water bomb. 'You know,' Udi smiled. 'Once, when I was little, before I met you, I used to come up here a lot and throw water bombs on people in the street below. I'd aim them into the space between that awning and the other one,' he explained, bending over the railing and pointing down at the narrow gap between the awning over the grocery store and the one over the shoe store. 'People would look up, and all they'd see was the awning. They wouldn't know where it was coming from.'

The angel got up too, and looked down into the street. He opened his mouth to say something. Suddenly, Udi gave him a little shove from behind, and the angel lost his balance. Udi was just fooling around. He didn't really mean to hurt the angel, just to make him fly a little, for laughs. But the angel dropped the whole five floors, like a sack of potatoes. Stunned, Udi looked at him lying there on the sidewalk below. His whole body was completely still, except the wings that were still fluttering a little, like when someone dies. That's when he finally understood that of all the things the angel had told him, nothing was true. That he wasn't even an angel, just a liar with wings.

SIDEWALKS

I arrived a week late like I always do. I never come on the actual date. I did go to the funeral and to the first memorial, but with all those people staring, the firm handshakes, your mother smiling at me teary-eyed and asking me when I was finishing my degree – I stopped coming. The date itself doesn't mean much to me anyway, though it's an easy one to remember: 12th December, the twelfth day of the twelfth month.

Ronen's sister is a doctor at Beilinssohn Hospital, and she was on duty right at the moment when your heart stopped. I heard Ronen tell Yizhar that you died exactly, but exactly, at twelve.

Ronen got all worked up about it: 'On the twelfth of the twelfth at twelve. D'you realize what a coincidence that is?' he whispered so loud that everyone could hear. 'It's like an omen from Heaven.'

'Incredible,' Yizhar muttered. 'If only he'd held out for another twelve minutes and twelve seconds, I bet they'd have issued a stamp in his honor, or something.'

It really is easy to remember – the date, I mean – and the street sign we stole together on Yom Kippur. And that idiotic boomerang they brought you from Australia, the one we used to throw in the park when we were kids and it would never come back. Every year I come and stand beside your grave and think back, remembering something else each time, remembering very clearly. We'd had five bottles of beer each, and after that you downed another three shots of vodka. I felt okay that night. A bit hazy, but okay. And you? You were stone drunk. We walked out of the pub in the direction of your house, a few hundred meters away. We were wearing those gray raincoats we'd bought together at the mall. Your walk was unsteady, and you bumped into a telephone pole with your shoulder. You took a step back and stared, not quite knowing what to make of it. I closed my eyes and the blackness of my lowered eyelashes mingled with the dark vapors of the alcohol. I tried to imagine you far away from me, in a different country, say, and the thought of it frightened me so much that I opened my eyes at once, only to see you taking another unsteady step, and falling backwards. I caught you just before you hit the ground and you smiled at me with your head tilted back, like a kid who's discovered a new game.

'We won,' you told me, as I helped you up. I had no idea what you were talking about. Then we took a few more steps and again you fell, deliberately. You just let your body drop forward, and I grabbed you by the coat collar, a tenth of a second before your face hit the sidewalk.

'Two to nothing,' you said, and leaned on me. 'We're so good, these sidewalks don't stand a chance.'

We kept walking towards your house, and every few meters you let yourself drop to the sidewalk, and every time it happened I'd catch you – by the belt, by the waist, by the hair. Not letting you touch the floor. 'Six to nothing,' you said, and then, 'Nine to nothing.' It was a cool game, we were really great. We couldn't lose.

'Let's keep them down to zero,' I whispered in

your ear, and that's just what we did. By the time we reached your house we'd scored an amazing twenty-one to nothing. We entered the building, leaving the humiliated sidewalks behind us. Your roommate was there in your apartment, sitting up and watching TV.

'We clobbered 'em,' you said as we walked in, and he rubbed his eyes behind his glasses and said we looked terrible. I was about to wash my face but before I could even reach the sink I threw up in the bathtub. I heard you screaming in the hallway that you weren't about to pee that way. I came out of the bathroom and saw you swaggering, with your pants down to your knees.

'I'm not going to pee with you holding me,' you told your roommate. 'You I don't trust. Only him. I want him to hold me,' you said, pointing at me. 'Only him.'

'It's nothing personal.' I smiled at the roommate. 'It's just that we've had lots of practice.' I held you up by the waist.

'You're simply crazy.' The roommate shook his head, and went back to his TV show. You finished peeing. I threw up again. On the way to your bed you fell once more, and I caught you, just barely, and then both of us fell to the ground. 'I knew you'd catch me,' you laughed.

'Look,' you said and tried to get up again. 'I'm not scared of falling any more, not at all.'

There are two kids here at your gravesite, aiming their tennis ball at the tombstones. I think I've figured out the rules: if the stone they hit is an officer's, they score a point. If it's a cadet's, it's a point for the cemetery. They hit your tombstone and the ball bounced right back towards my hand. I caught it. One of the kids walked up to me apprehensively.

'Are you the guard?' he asked. I shook my head. 'So will you give us our ball back?' He took another step in my direction.

I handed him the ball. He moved up closer to the tombstone, squinting a bit.

'SFC,' he shouted to his friend who was standing at a distance.

'What's SFC?' the distant one asked. The one with the ball shrugged. 'Excuse me,' he asked. 'Is SFC an officer or just an ordinary soldier?'

'An officer, of course,' I said. 'It stands for Supervisory First Commander.'

'Yeah!' he shouted and hurled the ball high in the air. 'Eight to seven.' His friend came running, and yelled, 'We beat the tombstones! We beat the tombstones!' and the two of them started jumping and yelling like they'd just taken the world championship at least.

WORLD CHAMPION

In honor of my dad's fiftieth, I bought him a gold-plated navel cleaner with *For the man who has everything* inscribed across the handle. It was a toss-up between that and *Axis of Evil – Axis of Hope*, and I debated a lot. My dad was in a good mood all evening, the life of the party. He showed everyone how he brushes his navel clean, and made sounds like a happy elephant. My mom kept telling him, 'C'mon, Menachem, stop it.' But he didn't stop.

In honor of my dad's fiftieth, the tenant who lives in the apartment above decided he wasn't leaving, even though his lease was up. 'Look, Mr Fullman,' he told my dad as he bent over a dismantled Maranz amplifier, looking like a butcher. 'In February I'm off to New York to open a stereo lab with my brother-in-law, and there's no way on earth I'm gonna move all my gear outta here just to find myself an apartment for two months.' And when my dad told him the lease was up in December, Shlomi-Electronics went right on working as if nothing had happened, and said in the tone you use to shake off the pest who tries to sponge some money off of you for a worthy cause: 'Lease-shmease, I'm staying. You don't like it? Then sue me,' and stabbed his screwdriver all the way through the innards of the amplifier.

In honor of my dad's fiftieth, I went with him to see his lawyer, and the lawyer said there was nothing to be done. 'Settle with him,' he suggested, rummaging through his drawer in a desperate search for something. 'Try to get another three–four hundred out of him, and leave it at that. A court case will only give you an ulcer, and after two years of running around you're still not sure to get any more than that.'

In honor of my dad's fiftieth, I asked him why we don't just go into Shlomi-Electronics' apartment at night and change the lock and dump all his stuff into the yard. And my dad said it was illegal, and that I shouldn't dare do such a thing. I asked him if it was because he was afraid, and he said he wasn't, he was just being a realist. 'Why bother?' he asked and rubbed his bald patch. 'You tell me, why bother? For another couple of months? Forget it, it's not worth the effort.'

In honor of my dad's fiftieth, I thought back about what he'd been like when I was a kid. Real tall, and working in the Municipality. He used to take me places. He'd carry me piggy-back. I'd yell 'giddyup', and he'd run up and down the stairs, with me on his back, like a crazy man. He wasn't a realist yet back then. He was the world champion.

In honor of my dad's fiftieth, I stood on the landing and looked at him. He was bald, he had a little potbelly, he hated his wife, who was my mom. People kept stepping on him and he'd tell himself it wasn't worth the effort. I thought of the son-of-a-bitch tenant stabbing amplifiers up there in the apartment that had belonged to my grandfather who was dead, and just knowing that my dad won't do a thing, because he's tired, because he's got no guts. Because even his son, who's only twenty-three, won't do a thing.

In honor of my dad's fiftieth, I thought about life for a second. About how it spits right in your face. About how we always give in to all kinds of assholes because they're not worth the effort. I thought about myself, about my girlfriend, Tali, who I don't really love, about the bald patch that's hiding under my hairline, about the inertia that somehow always keeps me from telling a girl I don't know on the bus that she's really pretty, from getting off at the stop with her and buying her flowers. My dad had gone inside already, and I was left on the landing by myself. The light went out and I didn't even turn it back on. I felt like I was choking. I felt like a flunky. I thought about my kids, who'd go scurrying like mice through an underground mall only to come back to me with *Axis of Evil – Axis of Hope*.

In honor of my dad's fiftieth, I whacked his tenant across the face with a wrench. 'You broke my nose,' Shlomi whimpered, writhing on the floor. 'You broke my nose.' 'Nose-shnose,' I lifted the Phillips screwdriver off his workbench. 'You don't like it? Then sue me.' I thought about my dad, who must be sitting in the bedroom now, cleaning his navel with a brush that has a gold-plated handle. It got me mad, it got me burning mad. I put the screwdriver away and added a kick in the head for good measure.

PAINTING

Say someone promises to make you a painting. Any painting, nothing specific. You let him have your apartment for a month and in return he'll make you a painting. You don't sign a contract or anything, but still it's a transaction like any other. Objectively speaking, it's a win-win situation. You take advantage of his enormous talent for painting, and he takes advantage of your much-appreciated talent for disappearing from the country for weeks at a time – to Thailand, to Japan, or in this case, to a solid destination, like France, for instance. Know what? Paris.

The big question to be asked now is whether the transaction is fair. It's legal, that's for sure, because there's mutual consent. But is it fair? To be honest, it's hard to say. You're sitting there, on the Champs-Élysées, sipping a small espresso, while he has to make you a painting like some slave. But on the other hand, the rent he would have to pay for a place like yours if he rented it for a month would be much higher than the best price he could get for any of his paintings. Still, the guy is shitting in your toilet, sleeping in your bed, covering himself with your blanket. Not just him, maybe all sorts of other people too, people he brings home with him, you haven't a clue. As for you, meanwhile, you're holed up in some tacky French hotel with a crabby receptionist who doesn't understand a word of English. All in all, that Champs-Élysées is nothing to write home about, with the July sunshine frying your brains and a million Japanese tourists. How are you ever going to last an entire month here? God only knows. A hypothetical God, of course, because all this doesn't really happen.

Say that two weeks into the deal you suddenly have to return home. Your wallet's been stolen, or maybe you only think it's been stolen but actually you lost it. It dropped, or you dropped it – same difference. You're out of money, and you're going home. The agreement said 'one month', and the question arises: do you have the right to go back to your apartment ahead of time? On the face of it, the answer is yes. But maybe not. Try to picture it the other way around. Suppose the other party in this transaction had lost his painting supplies. No, that's not a good analogy. Say he'd lost his talent. Would it still be fair of you to ask him to finish the painting? But the analogy, in this case, doesn't really work, because talent is such an elusive commodity, one you never just come across up close, whereas an apartment is a piece of property that's registered in the Housing Department, and French money is something that you can easily get from your parents. In any case, you're back, and you're both in the apartment; you in one bedroom and the other party in the other. At night you sometimes meet outside the bathroom.

The other party has a pretty face, and a body that really turns you on. Say you're very attracted to it. You're sweating. Know what? Let me make this easy on you: say the other party is a girl. A girl with a very attractive face and a body that turns you on. Here, let me open a window. Better now?

The other party is prettier. Prettier than the paintings she makes. Because pretty is what she is all the time, whereas painting is what she does only when she isn't sleeping or eating or fucking men you don't know on sheets you got from your parents for your birthday. Know what? On different sheets. But with men you do know. No, I won't say who, but some of them are even men who you know really well.

So where were we? Ah, the Champs-Élysées. You threw your wallet somewhere and went home. The two of you have worked it out. You each have a room. Except that in this particular case, her room is yours too. And the painting? It doesn't fucking appeal to her right now. Or maybe it does, except that you don't feel comfortable asking her about it. But all those men who keep coming and going in the middle of the night, they make her scream. And you, to you it seems very inconsiderate. Because if you had been able to fall asleep at night, it would have woken you up for sure. And what kind of a business is this anyway? Men you know, and I won't say who, make her scream in the middle of the night, and then in the morning she's got no energy left to make you the painting that the contract says she has a legal and moral obligation to deliver.

As far as you're concerned, it's clear enough, but what can you tell her? Get some sleep so you have enough energy left to make the painting you owe me? You'll never work up the courage, especially not when you came back two weeks ahead of schedule. Besides, maybe she is working on it, painting models, men you know. Like your older brother, for instance. In the middle of the night. And when he moves a little, she screams at him, that's how frustrated she is. What is she painting? You really ought to find out. You should know that the painting itself can tell you a lot about how she feels about you. Maybe she's really in love with you? Maybe this whole transaction with the apartment was just a pretext to get closer to you? Either way, would you kindly let go of your brother's neck? He's turning sort of blue.

So where were we? Blue. So in the end it turns out she was making you a painting of the sea. No, the sky. Sorry, you strangled your brother. Ah, yes, we were just saying that you can learn a lot about a person's character from a painting.

MY BROTHER'S DEPRESSED

It isn't like just anyone walked up to you in the street and told you he's depressed. It's my brother, and he wants to kill himself. And of all the people in the world, he had to tell it to me. Because I'm the person he loves the most, and I love him too, I really do, but that's a biggie. I mean, like, wow.

Me and my little brother are standing there together in the Shenkin Playground, and my dog Hendrix is tugging away at the leash, trying to bite this little kid in overalls in the face. And me, I'm fighting with Hendrix with one hand, and searching my pockets for a lighter with the other.

'Don't do it,' I tell my brother. The lighter isn't there, in either pocket. 'Why not?' my little brother asks. 'My girlfriend's left me for a fireman. I hate university. Here's a light. And my parents are the most pitiful people in the world.' He throws me his Cricket. I catch it. Hendrix runs away. He pounces on the kid in the overalls, pushes him flat on the lawn and his scary Rottweiler jaws clamp down on the kid's face. Me and my brother try to pry Hendrix off the kid, but he won't budge. The overalls' mother screams. The kid himself is suspiciously subdued. I kick Hendrix as hard as I can, but he couldn't care less. My brother finds a metal bar on the lawn, and whams it down on the dog's head. There's a sickening sound of something cracking, and Hendrix collapses. The mother is screaming. Hendrix has bitten off her kid's nose, completely. And now Hendrix is dead. My brother killed him. And besides, he wants to kill himself too. Because to him having his girlfriend double-cross him with a fireman seems like the most humiliating thing in the world. I think a fireman is pretty impressive actually, rescuing people and all that. But as far as he's concerned she could just as well fuck a garbage truck. Now the kid's mother is attacking me. She's trying to gouge out my eyes with her long fingernails that are painted with repulsive white polish. My brother picks up the metal bar and bangs her on the head, too. He's allowed to, he's depressed.

THE SAD STORY OF THE ANTEATER FAMILY

To Moshe

The whole town was actually one long avenue. Twenty houses on either side. In front of each house was a picket fence, and if you took a stick and ran it along so its tip bumped against the wooden slats, which made a god-awful racket, you could cross the whole town in one go. And this was what the kids actually did most of the time. If you started running north on the left side of the street, the last house, whose slats were the last ones, after which the stick would just glide through the air, belonged to Robin Schweig. Most of the kids preferred to run on the left side, because one of the houses on the right side belonged to Nehemiah Swan, who was a little crazy, and sometimes he would come out with his rifle and yell 'Turks!' at them, and threaten to shoot. But the best direction to run in was from north to south, because that way you'd end up at one of the two most interesting houses in town, and you'd have a pretty good chance of getting fed, too. One of them belonged to Eliyahu Beaver, who had pitch-black skin and curls that bobbed like springs, and the other, right across from him, belonged to the Anteater Family – Silky and Nehama Anteater and their son Ariel. Now, Silky Anteater wasn't just the nicest person in town – which nobody could deny – he was also the most exceptional. His body was covered with shiny fur, he had the most incredible nose, and he could dance so beautifully and tell funny jokes.

Friday evenings, they would all gather at the end of the avenue, and Eliyahu Beaver would take out an empty jumbo-size olive can and bang on it and make 'kha – kha – kha –' sounds as if he was about to choke, and Silky Anteater would break into a jig. It was a sight to behold. Every Friday he would do his dance and people never tired of it – of the way he moved, with his fur shining in the soft glow of the torches, and his tongue shooting out of his mouth, doing its little dance, as if it had a life of its own. The grown-ups would hoist the little ones up on their shoulders, to make sure nobody blocked the kids' view and everyone would clap to the beat. As soon as Silky and Beaver finished their performance, Birdie Greenberg would take out his violin and everyone would join in. When they did the circle dance, Silky would dance too, and the others would watch in envy as his big furry paws swaddled the palms of the dancers on either side of him. 'It's like wearing gloves,' the lucky ones would rhapsodize when it was over. 'It's so cool.'

Sometimes Eliyahu Beaver and Silky would also organize dance fests in the middle of the week, and everyone would stay out dancing till the crack of dawn, the little ones too. The town didn't have a school yet in those days. Nobody knew there was such a thing as a school, and nobody minded if the kids slept late the following morning.

Everything changed the day Alexander Mensch came to town. He arrived out of nowhere, of course. Because for the local people any place that wasn't in town was nowhere. They all knew there were other places, outside of the town, like Minsk or Eilat or the Turkish penal colony north of Izmir. Except that nobody had ever actually ventured there except maybe Nehemiah Swan. Alexander Mensch arrived in town around 10 a.m., and Elk Kasterstein, who at that very moment was running his stick along the slats, starting at Robin Schweig's house and heading south, bumped into him and accidentally pushed him into a puddle. Elk apologized and tried to help Mensch to his feet, but Mensch just stayed in the puddle, yelling at Elk and at all the kids that they were bullies and that they belonged in school, or in jail. He yelled so loudly that Nehemiah Swan came out and threatened to shoot him with his Muslim-slaying rifle unless he piped down. But not only did Mensch not stop yelling, he actually moved up an octave and started shrieking that he hadn't come all the way from Bern on foot just to have a gang of barbarians slaughter him like some animal. And Swan, who had the well-deserved reputation of being the most highly strung person in town, began to pour gunpowder into the chamber of his celebrated sentry rifle. Luckily for Mensch, his yelling woke Birdie Greenberg, who'd been sleeping late that day. Birdie grabbed the rifle out of Swan's hand, and even managed to get Mensch to calm down and helped him up out of the puddle. They took Mensch over to Robin Schweig's house, gave him a pair of dry trousers and made him some coffee with cream.

Mensch was horrified to learn that not only did the town he'd chanced upon have no name, it had no school either. Every civilized person, Mensch explained, would be shocked to hear such a thing, and it came as a shock to him in particular, as a renowned educator from Bern. He demanded that Birdie Greenberg call a meeting of the entire town that very day. It was Friday, and that evening everyone gathered at the edge of town. Beaver left his olive can at home, and Silky Anteater didn't dance. Everyone just stood around quietly and listened to Mensch, who talked for almost an hour. Mensch said they ought to announce a name for the town right away, and that a school had to be established, with himself as principal. Then he said 'Kultur' seven times and 'Levantines' three times and 'a disgrace' five times, and lots of other words and expressions in languages that nobody understood. When he finished talking, he gave the whole crowd a menacing stare, applauded himself, said 'Kultur' two more times and 'for the coming generations' once, and stepped down off the stage. He proceeded directly to Robin Schweig's house and the debate continued without him. In truth, it wasn't much of a debate. Birdie Greenberg and Swan were the only ones who spoke. Swan said they shouldn't let the Turk get the idea that they were afraid of him and that as far as he was concerned, they could shoot him like a dog, whereas Birdie Greenberg said they ought to do whatever Mensch recommended because if they didn't do exactly what Mensch said he would go on badgering them forever. In the end, they put it to a vote. Everyone abstained, because they just didn't understand what was happening, except Nehemiah Swan, who let it be known he was boycotting the whole thing, and Birdie Greenberg, who supported both of Mensch's proposals. The following morning, the town was officially given a name, and they started building a school where the barn used to be. Mensch proposed the name 'Progress' because he thought that a symbolic choice often spearheads the implementation of a desired reality, and everyone agreed with him because they had a very clear recollection of Birdie Greenberg's warning on the previous night. Birdie also prepared a large sign with the name on it, and stuck it at the southern entrance to the town. He promised to make another one for the northern side. All the others helped build the school, except for Swan who kept snooping around the old barn like a vulture and every now and then he'd lean on his old sentry gun and direct menacing gazes at Mensch.

Construction of the school went on for two weeks. Mensch announced there would be no parties during that time, so people wouldn't waste their energy, but he promised a cultural event when the building was completed. At the celebration marking the end of construction, Mensch informed Beaver that he was not to bang on his olive can, and Silky Anteater was not to dance, and instead he recited three poems by Schiller and one by Goethe, and played something by a dead Austrian on Birdie's violin, a tune that didn't lend itself to dancing. Then he made everyone go to bed because the next day was to be a work day and a school day and the start of a hallowed tradition of far-reaching changes in the town of Progress.

School started, and within a few weeks, people even began getting used to it. 'You can get used to anything, even smoldering embers between your toes,' said Nehemiah Swan, who still had vivid memories of his days in the Turkish prison. He'd come down to the schoolyard from time to time with his sentry rifle, but he was just going through the motions and didn't pose a serious threat. Unlike Swan, many people were actually rather pleased with the school because the kids no longer ran along the fences with their sticks, making a racket. Mensch divided up the school time by days: Mondays and Tuesdays were *Kultur* days on which the children had to memorize poems in unfamiliar languages. Wednesdays, Thursdays and Fridays were *Wissenschaft* days, devoted to the sciences. It was about three months after the school was built, on a Friday, the last *Wissenschaft* day of the week, that the sad story of the Anteater Family began.

Friday was Flora and Fauna Day, and Mensch always devoted it to the painstaking description of a particular plant or animal. That particular Friday, he walked in with a rolled-up poster, untied it and tacked it on the board. The students were taken aback to see the face of Silky Anteater smiling down at them from the poster. They didn't quite know how he was connected to their science class, but Mensch explained that the poster showed a lower form of animal, a four-legged mammal that eats ants. Ariel Anteater, who was sitting in the back row, got up and rushed out of the room, with tears in his eyes. An hour later he was back, with his father. Silky Anteater walked into the classroom, looking really mad.

'Mensch, I'd like a word with you,' he muttered.

'Not now,' Mensch insisted. 'In an hour, when class is over.' Silky Anteater nodded.

'Go back into class for now,' he told Ariel softly, and left the room. Ariel wanted to return to his seat, but Bambi Leibovitz wouldn't let him sit next to her.

'Yuck. I don't want you sitting here,' she said. 'Go outside and eat some ants with your repulsive father.'

Mensch told her off and she let Ariel sit down but moved her chair away, very deliberately. Mensch explained about the anteater's mating habits, and everyone gave Ariel a derisive stare.

'So your mother gets down on all fours, eh?' Fawn Deerborne whispered to Ariel. 'Is that how they made you?'

Looking out the window, the children saw Ariel's father sitting on the steps, staring at the ground.

'He must be looking for ants to eat,' Bambi said to Elk Kasterstein.

Ariel didn't answer; he just stared at the ground too. As soon as class was dismissed, they all ran outside. They kept as far away as they could from Ariel's dad, and Fawn Deerborne even swore at him when he was out of earshot. Ariel's dad didn't say a thing. He just waited for all the kids to leave, and then went inside to talk to Mensch.

'I don't understand, Mr Mensch,' Silky Anteater said, shaking his head sadly. 'Why are you doing this? Why are you teaching the children all those lies about me? Why are you wrecking my little boy's life?'

'Lies? Hah!' Mensch said, in a self-important, contemptuous tone. He took the poster and rolled it back up. 'What we have here are proven scientific facts collected by the finest scholars in the world . . .'

'Proven facts?' Silky Anteater interrupted him angrily. 'What kind of double-talk is that? Do I look to you like someone who walks on all fours? Do I eat ants? Are you serious?'

'Look, Mr Anteater, you cannot ignore the facts. You are covered in fur and you have an unusually shaped, long tongue, and besides, there's your name, Silky Anteater . . .'

'Birdie Greenberg is called "Birdie" but that doesn't mean you'll go teaching the kids that he flies through the air and shits on their heads,' Silky interrupted again. 'The things you're saying have nothing to do with facts. It's a bunch of crap, crap that's going to wreck my family's lives, but you don't give a damn. You don't give a damn about real life, all you care about is your lousy *Wissenschaft* and all those dead German poets from three centuries ago . . .' Silky Anteater stopped. He took a few deep breaths and wiped his eyes with the fur on the back of his paw. 'You keep interrupting me,' Mensch hissed in an angry, sanctimonious tone. 'You go out of your way to disregard my sensible statements. I don't see the point of pursuing this . . .' It wasn't Silky who interrupted Mensch this time, but the sound of kids screaming. Ariel's father rushed outside. There was a swarm of children jostling each other on the sand. Silky Anteater watched them in silence for a few seconds. His shadow happened to fall on Bambi Leibovitz, and when she caught sight of him, she sounded a warning. All the kids scattered and there was Ariel, lying in the sand, his pants pulled halfway down, his shirt torn. While his father was talking to Mensch, Ariel had been pushed to the ground by his classmates, and they had proceeded to stick ants under his clothing.

'Let's get out of here,' Silky Anteater said, taking Ariel's hand and helping him up. He took one final look at the school building. Through the open door of the classroom, he caught sight of Mensch tying the string around the rolled-up poster. 'Let's go home, son,' he said, laying his hand on Ariel's shoulder. 'There's nobody to talk to here anyway.'

They started walking towards the house. The tufts of fur on his father's arm felt good as they brushed against Ariel's neck.

THE MONKEY'S UNCLE

That night, Lukacz had another dream about himself in the jungle. Swinging from tree to tree, eating bananas, making it with all the she-monkeys. 'C'mon, you cowards,' he taunted the other monkeys, his luxuriant fur gleaming in the sunlight. 'C'mon, let Uncle Lukacz cook your goose.' But all the other males chickened out and lay low, because they knew better than to mess with Lukacz.

When Lukacz woke out of his dream he had a monumental headache. The sores on his body were stinging like hell. Some of them were oozing a viscous pus. He must have scratched them in his sleep again. He got out of his cage, locked the door behind him and headed straight over to Test Lab no. 3 (the skin cancer research lab). He was proud of where he worked. While most of the other animals took part in trivial experiments, like the ones in Labs no. 2 (cosmetics) and no. 4 (lazy eye), Lukacz was part of a truly important study. He arrived right on time for his 9 o'clock injection. The injector was Irena. 'Stop picking at those sores, Lukacz,' Irena said. 'It only makes things worse.' Lukacz stopped. Irena was his favorite lab assistant. 'Say,' he asked as she injected the stuff. 'Once the experiment is over and we find this cancer medication, d'ya think they'll agree to give me some time off? I miss the jungle like you wouldn't believe.' Irena withdrew the needle from his arm. He could see she was sad. 'Don't worry, Irena,' he tried to cheer her up. 'I won't be gone for long, you know me, I'm a sucker for work, I'll be climbing the walls before the month is up. Soon as I get back, I'll volunteer for the Alzheimer experiment, and that way we can still work together.' Irena gave him a hug and started to cry, and Lukacz didn't quite know what to do. 'Hey, I've got an idea,' he whispered, stroking the back of her neck. 'Why don't you take some time off and we'll do the jungle together. That way I could show you where I grew up. My family, the scenery. You'll have a great time. Everything is so green there.'

Irena didn't answer. She kept on crying, but slowly her sobs died down. When she'd finished crying, she let go of Lukacz, took a step back and smiled. 'Of course I'll come with you,' she told Lukacz. 'This year, they're going to have to give me some time off.' 'Wonderful,' Lukacz beamed, and looked into her eyes, which were still moist. 'It'll be terrific,' he promised. 'A whole new experience. You'll see.'

COCKED AND LOCKED

He's standing there in the middle of the alleyway, about twenty meters away from me, his kaffiyeh over his face, trying to provoke me to come closer: 'Zbecial Force Cocksucker,' he shouts at me in a heavy Arabic accent.

'What's up, *ya* Blatoon Hero? Your cross-eyed sergeant bush it up your ass too hard yesterday? Not strong enough to run?' He unzips his pants and takes out his dick: 'What's up, Zbecial Force? My dick not good enough for you? It was blenty good for your sister, no? Blenty good for your mother, no? Blenty good for your friend Abutbul. How's he doing, Abutbul? Feeling better, boor guy? I saw they bring in a zbecial heligobter to take him away. Like a crazy man he ran after me. Half a block he ran like a *majnun*. Blatsh!! His face squashed up like a watermelon.'

I pull up my rifle till I have him dead center in my sights.

'Go ahead and shoot, *ya* Homo,' he screams, unbuttoning his shirt and jeering. 'Shoot right here.' He points at his heart. I release the safety catch and hold my breath. He waits another minute or so with his arms akimbo, looking like he doesn't give a shit. His heart is deep under the skin and flesh, perfectly aligned in my sights.

'You're never going to shoot, you fucking coward. Maybe if you shoot, the cross-eyed sergeant won't go shoving it up your ass any more, eh?'

I lower the gun, and he makes another one of his contemptuous gestures. '*Yallah*, I'm going, Cocksucker. I'll bass by here tomorrow. When do they let you guard at these barrels again? Ten till two? See you then.' He starts walking off towards one of the back alleys, but suddenly he stops and smirks: 'Give Abutbul regards from the Hamas, eh? Tell him we really abologize for that brick.'

The rifle is back up in a flash, and I zero in till I have him right in my sights again. His shirt is buttoned up by now, but his heart is still mine. Then somebody knocks me down. I keel over in the sand, and suddenly I see Eli, the sergeant in

charge. 'Are you out of your mind, Meyer?' he
screams. 'What the hell do you think you're doing,
standing there like some damn cowboy with your
weapon smeared over your cheek? What do you
think this is? The fucking Wild West or something,
so you can go around putting slugs through
anyone who comes along?'

'Dammit, Eli, I wasn't going to shoot him. I just
wanted to scare him,' I say, avoiding his gaze.

'You want to scare him?' he yells again,
shaking me by the straps of my flak vest. 'Then
tell him ghost stories. What's the big idea –
aiming at him with your gun cocked, and the
safety off, no less?'

'Looks like Cross-Eyed isn't going to bush it up
your ass today, Homo,' I hear the Arab shout.
'Good for you, Cross-Eyed, punch him one for
me too.'

'You've got to learn to ignore them,' Eli says, out
of breath as he gets off me. 'Got that, Meyer?' He
switches to a menacing whisper. 'You've got to
learn to relax. Because if I ever see you pulling
anything like this again, I'm going to see to it
personally that they bring you up on charges.'

That night, somebody phoned from the hospital
to say that the operation hadn't gone so well, and
that Jacky would probably remain a vegetable.

'Just so long as we learn to ignore them,' I spit

out at Eli. 'If this goes on, we'll wind up ignoring them for good, like Jacky.'

'What's your beef, Meyer?' Suddenly Eli stands up straight. 'You think I don't care about Abutbul? He was as much my friend as yours, you know. You think I don't feel like taking the jeep right this minute and going from house to house and dragging them out and putting bullets through their fucking heads, every last one of them? But if I did that, I'd be just like them. Don't you get it? You don't understand anything, do you?' But suddenly I really do understand. Much better than he does.

He's standing there, in the middle of the alleyway, about twenty meters away from me, his kaffiyeh over his face.

'Good morning, Cocksucker,' he yells at me. 'Great morning,' I whisper back.

'How's Abutbul doing, Homo?' he yells at me. 'Did you give him regards from the Hamas?' I let my vest fall to the ground. Then I take off my helmet.

'What's up, Homo?' he shouts. 'Your brain all screwed up from so much fucking with Cross-Eyed?' I tear the wrapping off my field dressing, and tie it across my face like a kaffiyeh. The only thing still showing is my eyes. I take the rifle, cock it, and make sure the safety's on. I grab the butt with both hands, swing the rifle over my head a few times, and suddenly let go. It flies through the air, barely scraping the ground, then lands about midway between us. Now I'm just like him. Now I've got a chance of winning too.

'That's for you, *ya majnun*,' I scream at him. For a second he just stares at me, puzzled. Then he makes a dash for the weapon. He lurches right at it, and I race towards him. He's faster than me. He'll get to it before me. But I'll win, because now I'm just like him, and with the rifle in his hand, he'll be just like me. His mother and his sisters will make it with Jews, his friends will vegetate in hospital beds, and he'll stand there facing me like a fucking asshole with a rifle in his hand, and won't be able to do a thing. How can I possibly lose?

He picks up the rifle, with me less than five meters away, and releases the safety lock. One knee on the ground, he aims and pulls the trigger. And then he discovers what I've discovered in this hellhole over the past month: the rifle is worth shit. Three and half kilos of scrap metal. Totally useless. No point in even trying. I reach him before he so much as makes it up off the ground, and kick him hard, right in the muzzle. As he buckles over, I drag him up by the hair and pull off his kaffiyeh. I look him in the eye. Then I grab that face and bang it against a telephone pole as hard as I can. Again and again and again. So, Sbecial Force Cocksucker, who's gonna bush it up your ass now?

KORBI'S GIRL

Korbi was a punk like any other punk. The kind where it's hard to tell if they're more stupid than ugly or more ugly than stupid. And like any other punk, he had a good-looking girlfriend, the sort where nobody could figure out what she was doing with him. She was a tall brunette, taller than him, and her name was Marina. And whenever I'd walk by them on the street with my older brother Miron, I'd get a kick out of how he shook his head when we passed, in a slow side to side *No way*, as if he was saying to himself, 'What a waste, what a waste.' Korbi's girlfriend must have enjoyed those head-shakings too, because every time she saw us walking towards her and Korbi, she'd smile at my brother. Until it became more than a smile, and she began hanging out at our place, and my brother started kicking me out of the room. At first, she just came for short visits, around noon. But then she started hanging around for hours, and everyone in the projects was finding out about to it. Everyone except Korbi and his dumb sidekick Krotochinski, who used to spend the whole day on upside-down crates outside the Persian's grocery store, playing backgammon and drinking cherry soda. Like there was nothing more to life than those two things. They could sit around that board for hours, counting thousands of points of wins and losses that nobody cared about except them. Whenever you stood next to them you got the feeling that if the Persian didn't close his store in the evening or if Marina didn't show up, they'd be stuck there forever. Because except for Marina, and the Persian pulling the crate out from under him, nothing could have made Korbi get up.

It had been a few months since Korbi's girl started dropping by our place. And being kicked out of the room by my brother had become such a routine by then that I thought it would go on forever, or at least till he was drafted. Until the day my brother and I went to Teen Town. It was kind of far from our house in Ramat Gan, five kilometers maybe, but my brother insisted on walking instead of taking the bus, because he thought it would be a good warm-up for the Teen Town Soccer Dribbling Championship. It was getting dark, and we were both in our running suits, and as we passed the Persian's grocery store, we saw he'd just finished mopping and was pouring out a bucket of dirty water, so he could lock up.

'D'you see Marina today?' my brother asked him. And the Persian answered in a half-sucking kind of sound, that even without knowing Persian you could figure out meant *No*. 'Didn't see Korbi today either,' he said. 'First time this summer he didn't show up around here! I don't know why. It's a really nice day.'

We kept on walking. 'I bet he and Krotochinski are going to Teen Town too,' I said.

'What's it to me?' my brother hissed. 'What's it to anyone where they're going?'

But Korbi hadn't gone to Teen Town. I know, because we met him on our way there, near the artificial lake in the city park. He and Krotochinski were walking up the path towards us. Korbi was holding a rusty iron bar and Krotochinski was scratching his head. They didn't say anything, as though they were concentrating on something really important. We didn't say Hi, and they didn't either. And only when we were right next to them, when we'd almost passed them, did Korbi open his mouth. 'Son-of-a-bitch,' he said. And before I could figure out what was happening, he'd smashed the iron bar into Miron's stomach, and my brother fell onto the asphalt path, writhing in pain. I tried to get closer, to help him up, but Krotochinski grabbed me from behind.

'You,' Korbi said, turning Miron on his back with a few kicks. 'You stole my girl when I was her guy,' he screamed. His face was beet red, and before my brother could answer, Korbi had already pinned a shoe to his neck and shifted most of his weight onto it. I tried to break loose, but Krotochinski was holding me tight.

'You know, Gold. There's something in the Ten Commandments about what you did,' Korbi growled. '"Thou shalt not steal", it's called. "Thou shalt not steal." But you, you don't give a shit.'

'"Thou shalt not commit adultery",' I said. Don't know why. Down on the ground, I saw my brother's eyes shift.

'What'd you say?' Korbi snapped. As he turned towards me, the weight on my brother's throat lifted a little. He was beginning to cough and choke by then.

'I said that what you meant was "Thou shalt not commit adultery",' I mumbled. 'That it's a different commandment.'

73

I prayed to God that Miron would get to his feet
and beat the crap out of him.

'So what if it's a different commandment, what's
the difference? D'you think I'll take your asshole
brother's throat out from under my shoe?' He
shifted his weight forward again.

'No,' I said. 'That's not the reason, I mean. But
take your foot off of him, Korbi, you're choking
him, can't you see he can't breathe?'

Korbi took his foot off my brother's throat and
walked up to me. 'Say, Gold, you're pretty good at
school, aren't you? At least you have the face of
someone who's pretty good at school.'

'So-so,' I mumbled.

'Don't you so-so me,' Korbi answered and
rubbed the back of his hand against my face. I
threw my head back. 'You're an A student, aren't
you?'

Behind him, on the ground, I could see Miron
struggling to get up. 'So, tell me, Gold,' Korbi
said, bending over to pick up the iron bar. 'What
punishment does the Bible give a person who
disobeys a commandment?' I didn't answer. Korbi
started bouncing the iron bar in his hand. 'C'mon,
Gold.' He grimaced. 'Tell me, so I get it straight,
'cos I'm a moron and not as good in school as you
are.'

'I don't know,' I said. 'I swear, I don't know.

They just taught us the commandments, that's all. Nobody said anything about punishments.'

Korbi turned and looked down at my brother, who was still on the asphalt, and gave him a kick in the ribs. Not an angry kick but a casual one, like someone who's bored and starts kicking a Coca-Cola can. A tiny sound came out of Miron's mouth, like he didn't even have it in him to shout any more. I started to cry. 'Shit, Gold, stop crying,' Korbi said. 'Just answer the question.'

'I don't know, damn it,' I blubbered. 'I don't know what punishment you get for not doing what it says in the fucking commandments. Just leave him alone, you asshole, leave him alone.'

Krotochinski twisted my arm behind my back with one hand, and smashed me on the head with the other. 'That's for what you said about the Bible,' he hissed, 'and this,' he said, whacking me again, 'is for what you said about Nissim.' 'Let him go, Kroto, let him go,' Korbi sighed. 'He's pissed on account of his brother.'

Then, to me: 'Please just tell me, or I'm gonna smash your brother's knee.'

'Korbi, no,' I cried. 'Please don't.'

'So say it,' he said, waving the iron bar in the air. 'Tell me what God said was supposed to happen to anyone who steals someone else's girl.'

'To die,' I whispered. 'Anyone who disobeys that

commandment deserves to die.' Korbi drew the bar all the way back and threw it with all his strength. It landed in the artificial lake.

'D'you hear that, Kroto?' Korbi said. 'D'you hear Little Gold here? He deserves to die, and that,' he added, pointing towards Heaven, 'that's not anything I said. God said it.' There was something in his voice, like he was about to burst out crying too.

'C'mon, let's split,' he said. 'I just wanted you to hear Little Gold tell us who's right.' Krotochinski let me go, and they both left. Before they did, Korbi ran his warm hand across my face again. 'You're okay, kid,' he said. 'You're really okay.'

In the lot near the park I found someone who agreed to take us to the emergency room. Considering the way it looked, Miron got off lightly. An orthopedic collar for a couple of months and some black-and-blue marks. Korbi never came near Miron again, or near Marina either. She and my brother went out together for more than a year and then they broke up. Once, when they were still together, our whole family went on a beach trip. My brother and I sat on the sand and watched Marina play with our older sister in the water. We watched her splash water around with her suntanned legs, and looked at the long hair that almost covered her perfect face. And as we watched, I suddenly thought of Korbi, of how he'd almost cried. I asked my brother about that evening, when they caught us in the park, if he still thought about it, and he said he did. We were quiet for a while, watching Marina in the water. And then he answered that he thought about it a lot. 'Tell me,' I said. 'Now that she's with you, do you think what happened in the park was worth it?' My sister had turned her back to us and was shielding her head with her hands, but Marina just went on splashing and laughing. 'That night,' my brother said, slowing shaking his head from side to side. 'Nothing in the world is worth what happened that night.'

GOOD INTENTIONS

There was a thick envelope waiting in my mailbox. I opened it and counted the dough. It was all there. So was the note with the name of the mark, a passport picture, and the place where I could find him. I cursed. Don't know why. I'm a pro and a pro isn't supposed to do that, but it just came out. No, I didn't have to read the name, I recognized the guy in the picture. Grace. Patrick Grace. Nobel Peace Prize Laureate. A good man. The only good man I'd ever known. When it came to good men, there was probably nobody in the world that could match him.

I'd only met Patrick Grace once. It was at the orphanage in Atlanta. Like animals they treated us there. All year long, we wallowed in filth, they hardly fed us, and if anyone so much as opened his mouth, they let us have it with a belt. Lots of times they'd give you the belt without bothering to open the buckle. When Grace arrived, they made sure to get us cleaned up – us and that shit hole they called an orphanage. Before he came in, the director gave us a briefing: anyone who blabbered would be in for it later. We'd all had our share of his medicine, enough to know he meant business. When Grace entered our rooms, we were silent as mice. He tried talking with us, but we didn't really answer. Each boy got his present, said thank you and hurried back into bed. I got a dartboard. When I said thank you, he reached for my face. I cringed. Thought he was going to hit me. Grace ran his hand over my hair, gently, and without a word he lifted my shirt. In those days I used to shoot off my mouth a lot. Grace could figure that out by the look of my back. He didn't say anything at first. Then he said the name of Jesus a few times. Finally, he let go of my shirt and hugged me. While he was hugging me, he promised that nobody would ever hit me again. Needless to say, I didn't believe him. People don't just act nice to you for no good reason. I figured it had to be some kind of a trick; he'd be slipping off his belt any minute, and letting me have it. The whole time he was hugging me, I just wanted him to go. He went, and that same evening we got a new director and a whole new staff. From that time on, nobody ever hit me again, except that nigger I wiped out in Jacksonville. Did that one pro bono. Since then, nobody's lifted a finger on me.

I never saw Patrick Grace again. But I read about him in the papers a lot. About all the people he'd helped, all the good things he did. He was a good man. I guess there was no finer man anywhere. The only man I owed a favor on the whole face of this ugly planet. And in two hours I'm supposed to be meeting him. In two hours I'm supposed to be putting a bullet through his head.

I'm thirty-one. I've had twenty-nine contracts since I got started. Twenty-six of them I completed in one go. I never try to understand the people I kill. Never try to understand why. Business is business, and like I said, I'm a pro. I've got a good reputation, and in a profession like mine a good reputation is all that counts. You don't exactly place an ad in the paper or offer special rates to people with the right credit card. The only thing that keeps you in business is that people know they can count on you to get the job done. That's why I've made it a policy never to back out on a contract. Anyone who checks my record will find nothing but satisfied customers. Satisfied customers and stiffs.

I rented a room facing the street, right opposite the café. Told the owner that the rest of my belongings would be arriving on Monday, and paid two months' rent up front. There was half an hour to kill till the time I figured he'd get there. I assembled the gun and zeroed in the infra-red sight. Only twenty-six minutes left. I lit a cigarette. I was trying not to think about anything. Finished the cigarette, and flicked what was left of it into the corner of the room. Who'd want to kill a person like that? Only an animal or a complete wacko. I know Grace. He hugged me when I was just a kid. But business is business. Once you let your feelings in, you're finished. The carpet in the corner began to smolder. I got up off the bed and stepped on the butt. Another eighteen minutes. Another eighteen minutes, and it would be over. I tried thinking about football, about Dan Marino, about a hooker on Forty-Second Street who gives me head in the front seat of the car. I tried to think about nothing.

He was right on time. I recognized him from behind by that special bouncy walk of his, and the shoulder-length hair. He took a seat at one of the tables outside, in the best-lit spot, so that he was facing me head on. The angle was perfect. Medium range. I could take this shot blindfolded. The red dot showed on the side of his head, a little too far to the left. I corrected to the right till it was dead center, and held my breath.

Just when I had it all set, an old man wandered by carrying all his earthly possessions in a couple of bags – a typical tramp. The city's full of them. Right outside the café, one of the handles snapped. The bag fell to the ground and all his junk started spilling out. I saw Grace's body stiffen for a second, with a kind of spasm at the corner of his mouth, and right away he got up to help. He kneeled down on the sidewalk, gathering up the news-papers and the empty cans, and putting them back in the bag. The sight stayed fixed on him. His face was mine now. The red spot of the sight was floating on the middle of his forehead like a fluorescent Indian caste mark. That face was mine, and when he smiled at the old man, it glowed. Like the paintings of the saints on church walls.

I stopped looking through the sights, and took a good look at my finger. It was hovering over the trigger guard. Straight out, almost frozen. It wasn't going to go through with it. No point in fooling myself. It simply wasn't going to. I thumbed on the safety, and eased back the bolt. The bullet slid from the chamber.

I headed down towards the café with my gun in its case. It wasn't a gun any more really, just five harmless parts. I sat down at Grace's table, facing him, and ordered a coffee. He recognized me at once. Last time he saw me, I was an eleven-year-old kid, but he had no trouble remembering. Even remembered my name. I put the envelope with the money on the table, and told him that someone had hired me to kill him. I tried to play it cool, to pretend like I'd never even considered going through with it. Grace smiled and said that he knew. That he was the one who'd sent the money in the envelope, that he wanted to die. I've got to admit his answer caught me off guard. I stammered. Asked why. Did he have some malignant disease? 'A disease?' he laughed. 'Guess you could say that.' There was that little spasm again at the corner of his mouth, the one I'd seen through the window, and he started to talk: 'Ever since I was a kid I've had this disease. The symptoms were clear, but nobody ever tried treating it. I'd give my toys to the other kids. I never lied. I never stole. I was never even tempted to hit back in school fights. I was always sure to turn the other cheek. My compulsive good-heartedness just got worse over the years, but nobody was willing to do anything about it. If, say, I'd been compulsively bad, they'd have taken me to a shrink or something right away. They'd have tried to stop it. But when you're good? It suits people in our society to keep getting what they need, in return for a shriek of delight and a few compliments. And I just kept getting worse. It's reached the point where I can't even eat without stopping after every bite to find someone who's hungrier to finish my meal. And at night, I can't fall asleep. How can a person even consider sleeping when you live in New York, and sixty feet away from your house people are shivering on a park bench?'

The spasm was back at the corner of his mouth, and his whole body shook. 'I can't go on this way, with no sleep, no food, no love. Who has time for love when there's so much misery around? It's a nightmare. Try to see it from my point of view. I never asked to be this way. It's like a dybbuk. Except that instead of a devil, your body is possessed by an angel. Damn it. If it were a devil, someone would have tried to finish me off a long time ago. But this?' Grace gave a short sigh and closed his eyes. 'Listen,' he went on. 'All this money, take it. Go find yourself a position on some balcony or rooftop, and get it over with. I can't do it on my own, after all. And it gets harder every day. Even just sending you the money, having this conversation,' he mopped his forehead. 'It's hard.

Very hard on me. I'm not sure I'll have what it takes to do it again. Please, just pick a spot up on one of the rooftops and do it. I'm begging you.' I looked at him. At his tormented face. Like Jesus on the cross, just like Jesus. I didn't say anything. Didn't know what to say. I'm always armed with the right sentence, whether it's for the Father Confessor, for a hooker in a bar or for a Federal agent. But with him? With him I was a scared little kid again, at the orphanage, cringing at every unexpected move. And he was a good man, the good man, I'd never be able to waste him. No point even trying. My finger just wouldn't wrap itself around the trigger.

'Sorry, Mr Grace,' I whispered after a long while. 'I just . . .'

'You just can't kill me,' he smiled. 'That's okay. You're not the first, you know. Two other guys have returned the envelope before you. I guess it's part of the curse. It's just that you, with the orphanage and all . . .' He shrugged. 'And me getting weaker every day. Somehow I'd hoped you could return the favor.'

'Sorry, Mr Grace,' I whispered. I had tears in my eyes. 'I wish I could . . .'

'Don't feel bad,' he said. 'I understand. No harm done. Leave it,' he chuckled when he saw me pick up the tab. 'Coffee's on me. I insist. It has to be on me, you know. It's like a disease.' I pushed the crumpled bill back in my pocket. Then I thanked him and walked away. After I'd taken a few steps, he called me. I'd forgotten the gun.

I went back to get it, cussing quietly to myself. Felt like a rookie.

Three days later, in Dallas, I shot some senator. It was a tricky one. From two hundred yards away, half a view, side wind. He was dead before he hit the floor.

CLEAN SHAVE

She said shaving would do him good, so he shaved, specially for her. His complexion really shone in all its smoothness when he came to pick her up that night, and the fragrance of his after-shave was nice too. And they took in a movie and had a coffee somewhere, and then he drove her home. It was only their second date, so he didn't try anything, didn't even ask to come upstairs to her place. And as for her, before she got out of the car, she gave him a gentle little peck on his ruddy cheek. And he smiled awkwardly, and didn't kiss her back.

She was a girl worth biding your time for. A day would go by, and another, and eventually it would happen. A movie, a coffee, and another movie. One sunset, two bowling sessions, eventually she'd be his.

She said it was nicer with him shaved. The bristles hurt when they rubbed against her body. And now that they're together, where else would he put his face if not against her body? He couldn't think of anywhere better. He shaved every day, twice a day even. He cut off the bristles before they even started to grow in, letting the prickly skin burn with a kind of reddish warmth. Brushed his teeth all the time too: three times, four, five. Moving the toothbrush up and down and spitting into the basin, then rinsing with water, so there wouldn't be any toothpaste froth left. He felt so much better afterwards, more aesthetically pleasing, and once a week he even flossed. She wouldn't have minded kissing him without it, because she loved him, but no one could expect her to put her tongue in a place that smelled bad, or was dirty.

She said the eyebrows bothered her too. It was hard for her lips to slide down his forehead and kiss his eyes. The blade is the same blade after all, and as long as he was shaving anyway, would it really matter? Once a day, twice, sometimes even three times. And he flossed a bit more often too. Bought a whole roll, no bigger than a pack of cigarettes, but seventeen meters long. They rolled it very, very thin, like a sleeping bag that you manage to squeeze down till it's the size of a baguette. And while he was at it, he'd bought some after-shave too, in a quart-sized bottle, because he'd finished up the last one.

A long time went by. They'd been together for two months already. He just took care of his personal hygiene, and she took care of everything else. Didn't ask him to do so much as wash a glass. When it came to his chest and below, she didn't even have to say anything, he could tell at a glance. And as long as he was shaving with every meal, even more, he could do it all. Even eyebrows can sting the tongue of a person in love, someone who loves him smooth, with no corners, no sharp edges. Like all the others he'd met on her living-room floor, so nice and comfortable. At first he mistook them for pink beanbags. He'd seen her sitting on them many times, after all, looking very happy, so he sat on them too. It was so nice and smooth. How did they do it? he wondered, and they told him everything. The sharp edges were because of the bones, and there was this guy in Safed who could pull them right out, backbone and skull and all. It didn't really hurt. And she'd have it much nicer, which is all that counted really. Just her smile as she sat on him was worth everything.

BUBBLES

At night, after his wife fell asleep, he would go down to the car and count the bubbles on the windshield. On the car radio there would be quiz shows and people would answer and win prizes. Sometimes it was a Chinese meal, sometimes a make-up kit, nice prizes. He'd listen and count the bubbles on the windshield, unable to answer any of the questions. Deep inside, he was already dreaming about the lawsuit against Peugeot.

When he was young, he used to be good at quizzes. The programs were different then, and he used to phone in a lot. He knew all the answers, but most of the time the line was busy. He couldn't understand how come he used to know all the answers and now – nothing. He didn't know he had little snails inside his head that were drinking up his brain with a straw. Nobody knew. He'd caught it back in the army, on one of those educational field trips, from the water cooler at the Feldman Museum. There must have been a thousand people drinking from that water cooler, and they probably had snails too. Not that anyone noticed. It was one of those things that nobody notices: no pain, no symptoms, just bored little snails drinking up your brain.

There are lots of other things like that, all kinds of diseases that go undetected. His wife, for example, had been suffering for years from macramé spiders, which is much more common than snails, and more contagious too. They're transmitted in brochures and they settle in your soul, braiding it into dreadlocks. Wherever you had an emotional bond, they tear it out and replace it with a bead. His wife's soul looked like Bob Marley's head, and she had no emotions left. None whatsoever. And the only thing that made her cry was stuff she saw on TV. Nobody did anything about it. The doctors were so busy trying to keep up with her calcium and to make sure she didn't lose bone that they had no time left for nonsense. After all, she wasn't turning blue or anything, and she wasn't getting any lumps in her breasts either, she'd just stopped crying a little. Her husband even thought it was neat that the only thing that made her cry was what she saw on TV, because the things she saw there weren't real, so they couldn't do her any harm. It wasn't like bubbles on the windshield, where you could be driving along, and suddenly, bang! The whole window can go smashing into your face. He had counted five hundred and seventy-four by then and new ones kept showing up by the day. The music on the radio was so loud that you couldn't hear the snails burp. When it reaches six hundred, he thought, we'll file a lawsuit.

DINOSAUR EGGS

Uzi came to see me after school that day with a book about dinosaurs. He said that dinosaurs had died out but that you could find some of their eggs in different parts of the world, and that if we could find them, we'd have our own private dinosaurs and we'd be able to ride them to school and give them names. Uzi said dinosaur eggs are usually found in the corners of backyards, very deep in the ground. So we took a spade from the garden shed and started digging in the corner behind Natkovitz's balcony, where they build their *sukkah*. We dug for about two hours, till it started getting dark. We took turns, but we didn't find anything. Uzi said it wasn't deep enough and that

93

we'd have to keep going. Later, we went to wash our hands and faces under the faucet in the backyard and while we were washing up, Relly's boyfriend drove up on his beat-up motorcycle that's always breaking down.

'Hey, guys,' he said, trying to get on our good side. 'What's up?' Uzi elbowed me in the ribs. So I told him nothing was up and that we weren't doing anything. 'Not doing anything with a spade? Right. Where's your sister?' I told him she was probably inside, and he headed into the house. Relly loves the guy, but I can't stand him. It isn't anything he did. It's something in his face. There's something about it that looks like the bad guys in the movies.

'We have to go on digging at night,' Uzi said. 'Let's meet in the backyard at twelve o'clock sharp. You bring the spade and I'll bring a flashlight.'

'What's so urgent?'

'It's urgent, that's all,' Uzi answered, annoyed. 'Who's the dinosaur expert anyway, you or me? Dinosaurs are urgent business.'

In the end, I was the only one who showed up at twelve o'clock sharp, because Uzi's parents caught him trying to sneak out. I waited for him forever, I don't know how long, and just when I decided to give up and go home, Relly and the creep showed up. I was afraid they'd see me and ask questions. If I said anything about the dinosaurs, Uzi would never forgive me. I wasn't worried about them telling Dad on me, because if Relly said anything, she'd be in trouble too. Relly and the creep sat on the bench, right next to our hole, and suddenly the creep started doing things to her. He opened her clothes and stuck his hands inside, and all kinds of things, and she let him. I couldn't keep looking at them, so I told myself it was now or never, and I crawled away very quietly, back to the kids' balcony and from there to my own room.

We only dug in the daytime, I mean in the afternoon. Every day, except Saturdays, when Uzi's family went on trips. It went on for five months. We'd dug a really deep hole, and Uzi said we'd reached the center of the earth already and any minute now we'd be finding the dinosaur eggs. I'd pretty much stopped believing it by then, but it was much easier to dig than say so. I wanted someone to tell Uzi, but I didn't have the guts to do it myself. Relly, who used to play with us a lot, had almost stopped talking to me altogether, and when she did say anything, she called me Yossi, even though I hated that. Earlier, she'd spent all her time with the creep, but for the past two weeks, now that the creep wasn't coming around any more, the only thing she did was sleep all day and say she was tired. On Tuesday morning she even threw up in bed like a jerk.

'Yuck, you're gross,' I told her. 'I'm going to tell Mom.'

'If you breathe a word about this to Mom, you're dead,' she said in a serious voice, and it scared me a little.

Relly had never threatened me before. I knew it was all because of him, because of the creep with the beat-up motorcycle and the things he did to her. Lucky he stopped coming.

Two days after that, we found the egg. It was really enormous, the size of a melon.

'Didn't I tell you?' Uzi screamed. 'Didn't I tell you?'

We put it in the middle of the backyard and danced around it. Uzi said it had to be hatched now, we'd have to sit on it, so we did, for more than two months. In the end it hatched but instead of a dinosaur, there was a baby inside. We were very disappointed, because you can't ride a baby to school. Uzi said we had no choice, we'd have to tell my dad. My dad got all uptight, as soon as we walked up to him, before we even said anything.

'Where'd you get the baby from, eh?' he wanted to know. He kept on screaming, and every time we tried to explain he just yelled that we were liars.

Eventually, he bent over towards Uzi and grabbed him by the shoulder.

'Listen, Uzi, never mind Joseph,' he said, pointing towards me. 'He doesn't understand much, he's slow, but you're a smart kid. Tell me whose baby this is, who the parents are.'

'Well, we are, sort of,' Uzi said. 'Because we sat on it till the egg hatched, so we're like its father and mother.'

Dad gave Uzi a look like he was about to kill him, but then he turned around and I was the one who got slapped.

Dad took the baby to the hospital, and told me to wait for him in my room. It was noon by then, but Relly was still in bed.

'You're always sleeping,' I told her. 'You're like Sleeping Beauty.' Relly didn't say a thing and didn't move. 'I bet you won't get up till your Prince Charming comes,' I said, to piss her off, 'the prince on the beat-up motorcycle.'

Relly's lips moved, but her mouth didn't make a sound and her eyes stayed shut. 'He's the only one you'll get out of bed for,' I said. 'And if he gets a flat tire, you'll stay in bed forever.' Relly opened her eyes and I was sure she was going to get out of bed and whack me, but all she did was talk, and when she did, her eyes looked kind of sad.

'What do you want me to get up for, huh, Joe? To make my bed? To cram for my next exam?'

'I thought you might want to get up to see the dinosaur egg that Uzi and I found,' I said. 'It was supposed to be a scientific discovery, but in the end, it wasn't. I thought you'd want to see it.'

'You're right,' Relly said. 'A dinosaur egg really is something worth getting up for.' She pushed the blanket off with her feet and sat on the edge of the bed.

'You still throwing up?' I asked.

Relly shook her head and then she stood up.

'C'mon,' she said. 'Show me the dinosaur egg.'

'But that's what I was trying to tell you,' I said. 'That the egg was spoiled in the end, and it burst and Dad took it and he made Uzi go home and he slapped me.'

'Okay,' Relly said and patted me on the head. 'So let's go look for a different dinosaur egg, one that isn't spoiled.'

'Forget it,' I said. 'It'll just get Dad even madder. Let's go get a milkshake.'

Relly put on her sandals.

'And what happens if the prince on the beat-up motorcycle shows up the minute we go out?' I asked.

Relly shrugged. 'He won't be coming any more,' she said.

'But what if he does?'

'If he does, he'll wait for me.'

'Of course he will,' I said. 'How could he leave? His motorcycle never starts up anyway.' And as soon as I finished saying that, I started running. Relly ran after me, but we were all the way to the ice-cream stand by the time she managed to catch up. I ordered a double scoop with whipped cream and Relly got a strawberry milkshake.

HOPE THEY DIE

For Hanukkah vacation my parents sent me to a sleep-away camp for the whole week. From the minute I got there I hated it, and all I wanted to do was cry. The other kids were happy all the time. I couldn't figure out why, and it only made me want to cry even more. All day long I went from one activity to another and to the swimming pool with my lips pursed, not saying a word, so the kids wouldn't hear the tears in my voice and start picking on me.

At night, after lights-out, I waited a few minutes and then headed straight for the phone booth next to the dining room. It was raining outside, and I ran through the puddles barefoot, with just my pajamas on. The chill in the air caused my mouth to open, and out came these squeals that weren't even in my own voice. It scared the hell out of me. I dialed our home number, and Dad answered. All the way to the phone, I'd been hoping it would be Mom, but now, with the cold air and the rain and those squeals coming out of my throat, I didn't care any more. I told him to come and get me. And then the real crying started. He was a little mad, and asked maybe twice what was wrong, and then he let me talk to Mom. I just kept crying, couldn't get out a single word.

'We're coming to get you right away,' Mom said. I heard Dad mumble something and Mom snap at him in Polish. 'Did you hear me, Dandush?' she said again. 'We're coming to get you right away. Wait for us in your room. It's cold outside and you've got a cough. Wait for us in your room. Don't worry, we'll find it.'

I hung up and ran to the gate. I sat down on the curb and waited for them to come. I knew it would take them more than an hour. I didn't have a watch, so I kept trying different ways of counting in my head. I was cold and hot all at the same time, and they didn't come. By my calculation, I'd been waiting for more than two hundred years. The sun was starting to show and they didn't come. They said they'd come, the lying sons-of-bitches. I hope they die. I went on crying even though I didn't have it in me any more. Finally, one of the counselors found me and took me to the infirmary. They gave me a pill and I wouldn't talk to anyone.

At noon, this woman with glasses came in, and whispered something to the nurse. The nurse nodded and whispered back, loud enough for me to overhear: 'Poor little thing. He must have sensed it.'

The one with the glasses said something else to the nurse, and the nurse answered her out loud: 'For your information, Mrs Bella, I'm an educated woman, not some illiterate from the boonies, but there are things that even science can't explain.'

Then my older brother Eli came. He stood in the doorway looking kind of stooped and miserable, and kept trying to smile. After exchanging a few words with the nurse, he took me by the hand and we started walking towards the parking lot. He didn't even ask me to go get my stuff from my room.

'Mom and Dad promised to come and get me,' I said, half crying.

'I know,' he said, without looking at me at all. 'I know.'

'But they didn't!' I started to cry. 'All night long

I waited for them in the rain. Lying sons-of-bitches. I hope they die.'

And then he swerved all of a sudden and slapped me. Not one of those slaps you give a kid to make him shut up. He slapped me as hard as he could. I could feel my feet leaving the ground, and me going up in the air and then falling. I was in shock. Eli was one of those brothers that teach you how to throw a pass, not the kind that hit you. I got up off the asphalt. My whole body ached, and my mouth had the salty taste of blood. I didn't cry, even though my jaw hurt like hell. But suddenly Eli started.

'Damn it,' he said. 'Damn it, I don't know what the hell to do.' He sat down on the asphalt, crying. Then he calmed down a little and we drove back to Tel Aviv. The whole way he didn't say a thing. We got to the rented apartment where he was living. He'd just gotten out of the army and was sharing the place with someone.

'Your mom,' he said. 'I mean, our mom.' We were quiet for a minute. 'Mom and Dad, you know,' he tried again, and stopped. Finally we'd both had enough. I was getting really hungry because I hadn't had a thing to eat since yesterday, so we went into the kitchen and he made me a scrambled egg.

RAISING THE BAR

When Nandy Schwartz, the German pole-vaulter, cleared the six-sixty mark on the second try, he wasn't thinking of anything. There was a lump in his throat the size of a billiard ball, and as his eyes followed his outstretched feet passing over the bar without touching it, he struggled hard to keep from crying. He sank into the mattress below and was surprised at the enormous tears that were choking him as the announcer compared his record to that of the legendary Bob Beamon. 'Everyone here today has just seen a piece of history,' the megaphones crooned, and Nandy Schwartz, the only person in the stadium who hadn't really seen it, waved his arm high for the cameras.

Nandy's answering machine didn't say a thing. It just beeped with laconic arrogance – which didn't stop the Kellogg's people from leaving three messages.

'Raising the bar', was their suggestion for the new sales campaign, starring Nandy. 'Eight vitamins instead of six!'

Ninety thousand dollars in the bank. Nandy didn't hear the messages. He happened to be in the shower, curled up in the fetal position on the tiled floor, allowing the hot water to scald his back. The steam was seeping out of Nandy's singed pores like out of a rusty kettle, as he lay there with his thumb in his mouth, urinating into the stream of water, watching the yellow piss swirl towards the drain. Those ninety thousand dollars could fix him up, except that unfortunately he was already fixed up in his split-level five-room apartment in northern Bonn. Down on the tiled floor a piece of history was cooking away, sucking the memory of the many achievements out of a thumb. Apart from money, fame and health, he also had sixty-three girls, each with her own story, some with more than one. If he wanted to raise the bar any higher, his next lay would have to be a professor over fifty-three, and if he wanted to lower it, he'd have to find a retard under the age of sixteen.

THE REAL WINNER OF THE
PRELIMINARY GAMES

To Eyal

They used to talk a lot about life, about this and that: 'Yes – I'm happy; no – I'm not happy; I miss that girl; I want that job; I need a challenge.' Most of the time, they lied. Not on purpose, that's just how it came out, and after a while they both started getting tired of it. So they stopped all that, and moved on to other things, like the stock market and sports. Till Uzi came up with the idea of a four-beer test. It was simple: every three weeks they'd go into a pub and order four quarts of beer each. The first one they'd polish off without a word. After the second one they'd discuss how they felt, and the same after the third and the fourth. They'd always leave a big tip. Sometimes they'd throw up, the pub owners became used to it. Then Eitan went off to reserve duty for a month, and after that Uzi had this big project at work, so they wound up not meeting for six weeks. In those six weeks, Eitan grew a really cool little hippie-style beard and Uzi managed to stop smoking three times.

'We'll have to order eight beers each today,' Uzi said as they went into the pub, 'to make up for lost time.'

Eitan smiled. They weren't big drinkers, and even four quarts of beer was far too much. The TV in the pub was switched on, but without the sound. They were showing the highlights of the prelims in the Commonwealth Games.

'Get a load of the Brit, how happy he looks,' Uzi laughed and pointed at a scrawny figure jumping up and down on the screen. 'What's he getting so worked up about? All he did was come in first in his heat in the pre-prelims of some godforsaken race, the pre-Eurovision of track and field. The way he's carrying on you'd think he'd won at least three platinum Olympic medals.'

'The Europeans don't stand a chance in the

Olympic long-distance runs. The Africans are making mincemeat out of them,' Eitan said, 'so all they have left is the Commonwealth competitions.'

'All right,' Uzi insisted, 'but just because he hasn't got a chance of scoring at the Olympics, is that any reason to be so happy? Besides, he hasn't actually won anything yet, it's only the prelims.'

They downed the first beer, then the second. Uzi asked Eitan about his stint in the reserves and Eitan said it had been okay. Eitan asked him how the project had gone. 'Okay,' Uzi said. 'Okay, really. But for the past two months I've been feeling kind of burned-out at work. I come in without the old get-up-and-go, I work without the old get-up-and-go, I go home without the old get-up-and-go, you know.'

They drank their third beer and Eitan said that's how it was, it happens to everyone from time to time. He could hold down his liquor much better than Uzi. Whenever anyone threw up, it was usually Uzi. According to the rules, Uzi was supposed to say something too, but he didn't. He just sponged a cigarette off the waitress, lit up and stared at the screen. It was some entertainment show, with Dolly Parton and Kenny Rogers. Eitan kidded him about how he could ask the barman to turn up the volume. Uzi didn't even answer.

'I thought you said the acupuncture did you some good,' Eitan said, looking at Uzi, who'd smoked his cigarette down to a butt, and was holding what was left of it, trying not to burn his fingers.

'That Weiss is a con artist,' Uzi hissed. 'The acupuncture wasn't worth shit.'

It was a cheap fag, no filter. Uzi took one big final drag and it vanished like magic. He didn't even have to put it out or anything, there was simply nothing left. They downed the fourth pint. Eitan barely managed to finish, he was feeling sick as hell. Uzi was actually looking cool and asked the waitress for another cigarette.

'Tell you something,' Uzi said, once that cigarette had vanished too, 'I've had it.'

'With the cigarettes?'

'With everything.' Uzi pushed down hard on the ashtray, like he was trying to extinguish his finger too. 'With everything. None of it means anything, none of it. You know how it feels when you're somewhere and you ask yourself what you're doing there? That's how it is with me all the time, can't wait to leave. To go from wherever I am to some other place. There's no end to it, I swear to you, I'd have killed myself long ago but I'm too chicken.'

'Cut it out,' Eitan tried. 'That isn't you talking, it's the beer. Tomorrow morning you're going to wake up with a hell of a hangover and say that everything you said today was crap. Who knows? You might even decide to quit smoking again.'

Uzi didn't laugh. 'I know,' he muttered. 'I know it's the beer talking and that tomorrow I'll sound different. I thought that was the whole idea.'

They took a cab home. The first stop was Uzi's house.

'Take care of yourself, will you,' Eitan said and gave him a hug before he got out of the cab. 'Don't do anything stupid.'

'Don't worry.' Uzi smiled. 'I'm not going to kill myself or anything. I don't have the guts. If I did, I'd have done it a long time ago.'

Next, the cab dropped Eitan at his place, and he went upstairs. He had a gun in the drawer. He'd bought it with sportswear store coupons he'd received when he was an officer. Not that he was trigger-happy or anything, but it was either that or signing for an M-16 every time he went on leave. Eitan took the gun out of his underwear drawer and cocked it. He held it up to his chin.

Someone had told him once that if you shoot from underneath it wipes out your brain stem. When you shoot at the temple, the slug could go right through and you'd wind up a vegetable. He released the firing pin.

'If I want to, I can shoot,' he said out loud. He ordered his brain to pull the trigger. His finger obeyed, but stopped halfway. He could do it, he wasn't scared. He just had to make sure he wanted to. He thought about it for a few seconds. Maybe in the general scheme of things he couldn't find any meaning to life, but on a smaller scale it was okay. Not always, but a lot of the time. He wanted to live, he really did, and that's all there was to it. Eitan gave his finger another order to make sure he wasn't conning himself. It still seemed prepared to do whatever he wanted. He put the gun on half cock and pushed the firing pin back in. If it hadn't been for those four beers, he'd never even have tried it. He would have made up an excuse, said it was just a dumb test, that it didn't mean anything, but like Uzi said, that was the whole idea. He put the gun back in the drawer and went into the bathroom to throw up. Then he washed his face and his head in the sink. Before drying himself, he took a look in the mirror. A skinny guy, with wet hair, a little pale, like that runner on TV. He wasn't jumping or yelling or anything, but he'd never felt this good.

A FOREIGN LANGUAGE

For his fifty-first birthday we bought Dad a pipe. Dad said thanks, ate a piece of the cake that Mom had baked, and kissed everyone. Then he went into the bathroom to shave. He was one of those fanatical shavers, who go over each section three times, and emerge perfectly smooth, and without a nick. In my entire life I've never seen Dad nick himself even once.

Some people know French or Italian, all kinds of languages that they studied by correspondence or in courses run by the consulate. Take my older brother, he studied German once at the Goethe Institute. You never know when a foreign language might come in handy. Not only on trips abroad, sometimes it could actually save your life. My mother in the Holocaust and the German language, for instance, is a good example.

Once my father had finished going over each section of his face three times, he started on the back of his head. The razor wasn't built for that, and he had to spend half the time pulling out the thick hairs that got in the way of the blades. It was a hard and thankless task, and he was dying to call me into the bathroom to tell me about it. He wanted to tell me something, about how if he hadn't married my mother he would definitely have gone to Scandinavia and built himself a cabin in some godforsaken forest, and sat on his balcony every evening, smoking his pipe.

My girlfriend once asked me to tell her I loved her in a different language, an exotic one. And no matter how hard I tried and tried and thought and thought I just couldn't think of a thing. 'Hebrew isn't good enough?' I tried. 'Pig Latin? Atin-lay ig-pay? What if I say it twice? If I really and truly mean it?' It wasn't good enough. It didn't do it for her, and she just went on and on screaming, she can be that way sometimes. In the end she threw a heavy ashtray at my head, one with an insurance company logo on the side, and I had blood running down my forehead. 'Love me, love me,' she yelled. And I tried as hard as I could to think back over the things that the Russian guys at work had taught me, but the only thing that came into my head was swearwords.

Dad went over the back of his head five times. When he was through, and ran his hand over it, it was at least as smooth as his cheeks. The reason he wanted to build the cabin in a forest in Scandinavia was mainly because of the quiet. My dad was very partial to quiet. When my brother and I cried as children it bugged him so much that sometimes he just felt like strangling us. My dad took a can of special glue and a thin piece of wood like a popsicle stick from under the sink. He dipped the stick in the tin can and started spreading glue over the back of his head. It was a complicated procedure, because he couldn't see the surface he was covering, which is like spreading butter over a slice of bread when it's facing down. But my father didn't lose his cool, and kept spreading the sections of the back of his head very patiently and with the utmost precision. While he was doing it, he hummed a Hungarian ditty that went more or less like this: 'Ozo sep? Ozo sep? Okineko seme kek. Okineko seme fakete.'

'Who's the most beautiful? Who's the most beautiful? The one with the dark eyes. He's the most beautiful.' And after the ashtray on the head she left me. To this day I have no idea why. But to learn from something, you don't always have to understand it. Learn something important. My mother, for example, told the German officer not to kill her. She'd make it worth his while, because if he didn't kill her she'd sleep with him. Which was far less common than rape in those days. And then, when they were doing it, she pulled a knife out of her belt and slashed his chest open, just like she used to open chicken breasts to stuff them with rice for the Sabbath meal.

My father put the plug in the bathtub and turned on the water, not too hot and not too cold. Just right. Then he lay down in the bathtub holding his neck up above the water, and reached for the faucets, like so, lying on his back. The faucets were too high. My father relaxed his neck muscles and let the back of his head stick to the bottom of the bathtub. He did everything he could to lift up his head but he couldn't. The flier that came with the glue promised that no amount of water in the world would succeed in dissolving it. And the plug – he was wearing shoes. Let's see you pull a plug with your shoes on. Meanwhile, in my room, my brother and I were having an argument. I said Dad really liked his present, my brother said he didn't. We couldn't arrive at a clear conclusion, because with my father, you never know. *Bloo-bloo-bloo*, the water in the bathtub murmured in Scandinavian. 'Nur Gott weiss,' my brother said, showing off his German. 'Nur Gott weiss.'

DROPS

My girlfriend says someone in America invented a medicine against feeling alone. She heard about it yesterday on *Nightline*, and now she's sending a special delivery letter to her sister to ask her to mail her a crate of it. On *Nightline* they said that all the retail chains on the East Coast were selling it already and that in New York it was a big hit. It came in two forms, drops and spray can. My girlfriend asked for the drops. Just because she doesn't want to feel alone, there's no reason to harm the ozone layer.

You put the drops in your ear, and within twenty minutes you stop feeling lonely. It works on some chemical thing in your brain, they said on the radio, but my girlfriend couldn't follow. She's not exactly Marie Curie, my girlfriend. She's kind of dumb, even. Sits around the whole time thinking I'm going to cheat on her and leave her and all that. But I love her, I love her like crazy. Now, she says when she gets back from the post office, she doesn't have to live with me any more. Because the drops will be here any day, and she's not afraid of being alone any more.

Leave me? I say. For some drops? Why? But I love her, I love her like crazy. Move out if you want, I tell her, but for your information, no stinking eardrops are going to love you the way I love you. Except that eardrops won't ever cheat on her either. That's what she says, and then she leaves. As if I would.

She's rented a loft downtown, and now she waits for the mailman every day. Me, the mail doesn't do it for me, and I don't have any friends in other countries who'll send me things anyway. If I did, I'd have gone to them a long time ago. I'd go out drinking with them and I'd tell them my troubles. I'd hug them a lot and I wouldn't be embarrassed to cry next to them and stuff. We could spend years that way, our whole life. A hundred per cent natural, much better than drops.

SHOES

On Holocaust Commemoration Day, our teacher, Sarah, took us on the no. 57 bus to the Vohlin Memorial Museum and I felt really important. All the kids in my class had families that came from Iraq, except me and my cousin and one other kid, Druckman, and I was the only one whose grandfather died in the Holocaust. The Vohlin Memorial Museum was a really fancy building, all covered in expensive-looking black marble. It had a lot of sad pictures in black and white and lists of people and countries and victims. We paired up and walked along the wall, from one picture to the next, and the teacher said not to touch, but I did. I touched one of them, a cardboard photograph of a pale and skinny man who was crying and holding a sandwich. The tears running down his cheeks were like the stripes on an asphalt street, and Orit Salem, the girl I was paired up with, said she'd tell the teacher on me. I said that as far as I was concerned, she could tell everyone, even the principal, I didn't care. That was my grandfather, and I could touch whatever I wanted.

After the pictures, they took us into a big hall and showed us a movie about little kids being loaded onto a truck. They all choked on gas in the end. After that this skinny old guy came up on the stage and told us how the Nazis were scum and murderers and how he got back at them and even strangled a soldier to death with his bare hands.

Djerbi, who was sitting next to me, said the old man was lying, and from the looks of him, there wasn't a soldier in the world he could beat up. But I looked into the old man's eyes and I believed him. There was so much anger in them that all the attacks from all the hot-shot punks in the world seemed like small change by comparison.

In the end, after he was finished telling us about what he'd done in the Holocaust, the old man said that everything we'd heard was important, not just for the past but for what was happening now, too. Because the Germans were still living, and they still had a country. The old man said he'd never forgive them and he hoped we wouldn't either, and that we should never ever visit their country, God forbid. Because when he and his parents had arrived in Germany fifty years ago everything looked really nice and it ended in hell. People have a short memory sometimes, he said, especially for bad things. They prefer to forget. But don't you forget. Every time you see a German, remember what I told you. And every time you see anything that was made in Germany, even if it's a TV, because most of the companies that make TVs, or anything else, are in Germany, always remember that the picture tube and other parts underneath the pretty wrapping were made out of the bones and skin and flesh of dead Jews.

On our way out, Djerbi said again that if that old man had strangled so much as a cucumber, he'd eat his T-shirt. And I thought it was lucky our fridge was made in Israel, 'cos who needs trouble.

Two weeks later, my parents came back from abroad and brought me a pair of trainers. My older brother had told my mother that's what I wanted, and she bought the best ones. Mom smiled when she handed them to me. She was sure I didn't know what was in the bag. But I could tell right away by the Adidas logo. I took the shoebox out of the bag and said thank you. The box was rectangular, like a coffin. And inside it lay two white shoes with three blue stripes on them, and on the side it said Adidas Rom. I didn't have to open the box to know that. 'Let's try them on,' Mom said, pulling the paper out. 'To see if they fit.' She was smiling the whole time, she didn't realize what was happening.

'They're from Germany, you know,' I told her and squeezed her hand hard.

'Of course I know,' Mom smiled. 'Adidas is the best make in the world.'

'Grandpa was from Germany too,' I tried hinting.

'Grandpa was from Poland,' Mom corrected me. She grew sad for a moment, but it passed right away, and she put one of the shoes on my foot and started lacing it up. I didn't say anything. I knew by then it was no use. Mom was clueless. She had never been to the Vohlin Memorial Museum. Nobody had ever explained it to her. And for her, shoes were just shoes and Germany was really Poland. So I let her put them on my feet and I didn't say anything. There was no point telling her. It would just make her sadder.

After I said thank you one more time and gave her a kiss on the cheek, I said I was going out to play. 'Watch it, eh?' Dad kidded from his armchair in the living room. 'Don't you go wearing down the soles in a single afternoon.' I took another look at the pale shoes on my feet, and thought back about all the things the old man who'd strangled a soldier said we should remember. I touched the Adidas stripes again, and remembered my grandpa in the cardboard photograph. 'Are the shoes comfortable?' Mom asked. 'Of course they're comfortable,' my brother answered instead of me. 'Those shoes aren't just some cheap local brand, they're the very same shoe that Kroif used to wear.' I tiptoed slowly towards the door, trying to put as little weight on them as possible. I kept walking that way towards Independence Park. Outside, the kids from Borochov Elementary were forming three groups: Holland, Argentina and Brazil. The Holland group was one player short so they agreed to let me join, even though they usually never took anyone who didn't go to Borochov.

When the game started, I still remembered to be careful not to kick with the tip, so I wouldn't hurt Grandpa, but as it continued, I forgot, just like the old man at the Vohlin Memorial Museum said people do, and I even scored the tiebreaker with a volley kick. After the game was over I remembered and looked down at them. They were so comfortable all of a sudden, and springier too, much more than they'd seemed when they were still in the box. 'What a volley that was, eh?' I reminded Grandpa on our way home. 'The goalie didn't know what hit him.' Grandpa didn't say a thing, but from the lilt in my step I could tell he was happy too.

MY BEST FRIEND

My best friend peed on my door last night. I live in a fourth-floor rented walk-up. Dogs do that sometimes, to mark territory, to keep other males away. But he's no dog, he's my best friend. And besides, it's not his territory, it's the door to my apartment.

A few minutes earlier my best friend had been waiting for the bus. He didn't know what to do. Slowly his bladder started to get the better of him. He tried to fight it, reminding himself the bus would be there any minute, except that was what he'd reminded himself twenty minutes before. Then it suddenly occurred to him that I, his best friend, lived just a few blocks away, at

14 Zamenhoff, in a fourth-floor rented walk-up. He left the bus stop and started walking towards my apartment. Not exactly walking really, more like half-running, then breaking into a sprint. And with every step he was finding it more difficult to hold it in, till he thought of sneaking into someone's backyard and peeing against a wall or a tree or a gas tank. He was less than fifty meters away from my house when he got that idea, but it seemed kind of crude and very wimpy. There are a lot of bad things you can say about my best friend, but one thing he isn't is a wimp. So he forced another fifty meters and then started climbing the four floors to my place. With every step his bladder was getting bigger and bigger, like a balloon about to burst.

When he finally made it up all the stairs, he knocked on my door, then rang the bell. Then knocked again. Hard. I wasn't home. Now of all times, when he needed me so badly, I, his best friend, had preferred to go off to some pub, hanging out at the bar and coming on to every chick that came along. My best friend was standing there at the door, utterly desperate, he'd trusted me blindly, and now it was too late. He'd never make it all the way down those four flights. The only thing left for him to do afterwards was to leave me a crumpled note saying 'Sorry'.

Soon as she saw the puddle, the girl who'd agreed to come home with me that night had second thoughts. 'Number one,' she said, 'it's gross. I'm not stepping in that. Number two, even if you mop it up, the smell of it is all over the house by now. And number three,' she added with an ever-so-slight twitch of the lip, 'if your best friend pees on your door, that says something.' And after a short silence, she added: 'About you.' And after another silence: 'Not anything good.' Then she left. She was the one who told me that was how dogs marked territory. When she said it, she paused a little after the word 'dog', and gave me a meaningful look, from which I was supposed to grasp that my best friend had a lot in common with a dog. After that look, she left. I brought a floor-rag from the kitchen porch, and a pail of water, and as I mopped it up, I hummed 'We Shall Overcome'. It made me damn proud to know I'd managed to keep from slapping her one.

THE STUFF THAT DREAMS
ARE MADE OF

The shelves around us were packed full of the stuff that dreams are made of. Six hundred regular-size boxes, one hundred and eighty jumbo packs and three thousand disposable vials. It was dark. Night. Amir Meiri was standing behind the counter crying like a baby. 'We've had it,' he said. 'Keret, we're finished.' I felt terribly sorry for him right then. He had no future. He didn't even have a near present. I tried to imagine him five minutes from now, and there was nothing, just nothing. To tell the truth, if I'd tried the same trick on myself, I would've seen darkness too. As a fifty per cent partner in the business, my neck was in the same noose.

We first came across the stuff in Ko-Samui. Some Thai sold us a tube for twenty baht and we were sure it was suntan lotion. When the Thai saw Amir spreading it on his shoulders, he went completely crazy. 'No good, no good,' he yelled in his broken English, waving his hands. 'Put on eyes,' he said, pointing to his eyes. 'Only on eyes.' Amir did what he said and spread a little on his lids. So did I. 'Now you close eyes and dream,' the Thai ordered us. We closed our eyes. We stayed awake, but the dreams came. We weren't sleeping; they just came. Not hallucinations or anything, just pure dreams. Amir's first dream was about importing that stuff to Israel, making a bundle and buying a red Mazda sports car. I dreamt about you telling me on the phone that our last conversation before I left was a mistake, that I'm the one you really love, and it's that law intern who means nothing. That you were confused in that phone conversation, but now you understand. That you miss me so much. And that I didn't have to go to Thailand at all.

We opened our eyes; Ko-Samui was still there. 'Very good, yes?' the Thai asked. We bought the whole crate from him. We stayed in Ko-Samui two more weeks, two weeks of mentally editing scenes of how I come back to you and how everything is fine. I arranged them in sequence. When the hug comes, when we cry partly out of happiness, when that shyster comes to move his stuff out of the apartment and I'm so nice to him, get him a glass of juice, help him tie the double mattress on the roof of his Peugeot. Amir sat next to me the whole time, making calculations in a notebook. 'We'll be millionaires,' he said every few minutes. 'The big daddy of millionaires. The lottery is a welfare office compared to what we'll have in our wallets.'

And now we're here and Amir is crying like a baby. 'It's gone,' he mutters, banging the counter. 'All the money we had is gone.' Not to mention the money we didn't have. 'How could we have known?' he asks. 'How could we have known that the stuff only worked on us? It's not fair, it's just not fair.'

I don't know how come, but that's how it was. The stuff worked like magic on us, but didn't do a thing for other people. They spread the cream on their eyelids and waited, but nothing came. They could just as easily have used hummus. It only brought dreams to Amir and me.

At some point, Amir stopped crying and fell asleep just like he was, half lying there with his head on the counter. I took the invitation to your wedding out of my pocket. 'That Thai son-of-a-bitch,' Amir muttered in his sleep. 'Fucking asshole. He really screwed us.' I put the invitation back in my pocket, then went and took a jumbo jar off a shelf. I spread a thick layer on my closed eyelids and waited. Nothing happened. It could just as easily have been hummus. But I decided to keep my eyes shut anyway. I thought about the intern – pardon me, he's a lawyer now – who was awfully nice when I went to see both of you at home. I remembered how he helped me carry my things downstairs. 'I hope he drops dead,' Amir hissed into the Formica. 'Let him drop dead, amen. I'll bring beer and pretzels to his funeral.'

CRAMPS

That night I dreamt that I was a forty-year-old woman, and my husband was a retired colonel. He was running a community center in a poor neighborhood, and his social skills were shit. His workers hated him, because he kept yelling at them. They complained that he treated them like they were in basic training. Every morning I'd make him an omelet, and for supper a veal cutlet with mashed potatoes. When he was in a decent mood, he'd say the food tasted good. He'd never clear the table. Once a month or so, he'd bring home a bouquet of dead flowers that immigrant kids used to sell at the intersection where the lights were really slow.

That night I dreamt that I was a forty-year-old woman, and that I was having cramps, and it's night-time, and suddenly I realize I'm all out of tampons, and I try to wake my husband, who's a retired colonel, and ask him to go to the all-night pharmacy or to drive me there at least, because I don't have a driver's license, and even if I did, he still has an army car, and I'm not allowed to drive it. I told him it was an emergency, but he wouldn't go, just kept mumbling in his sleep, saying the meal was lousy, and that if the cooks thought they were getting furlough, they could just forget it, because this was the army and not some fucking summer camp. I stuffed in a folded tissue, and tried lying on my back without breathing, so it wouldn't leak. But my whole body hurt, and the blood was gushing out of me, sounding like a broken sewage pipe. It leaked over my hips, and my legs, and splashed over my stomach. And the tissue turned into a wad that stuck to my hair and my skin.

That night I dreamt that I was a forty-year-old woman and that I was disgusted with myself, with my life. With not having a driver's license, with not knowing English, with never having been abroad. The blood that had dripped all over me was beginning to harden, and I felt like it was a kind of curse. Like my period would never end.

That night I dreamt that I was a forty-year-old woman, and that I fell asleep, and dreamt I was a twenty-seven-year-old man who gets his wife pregnant again, and then finishes medical school and forces her and the baby to join him when he goes to do his residency abroad. They suffer terribly. They don't know a word of English. They don't have any friends, and it's cold outside, and snowing. And then, one Sunday, I take them on a picnic and spread out the blanket on the lawn, and they take the food from their picnic baskets and put out the food they've brought. And after we finish eating, I take out a hunting rifle and I shoot them like dogs. The policemen come to my house. The finest detectives in the Illinois police force try to get me for murder. They put me in this room, they yell at me, they won't let me smoke, they won't let me go to the bathroom, but I don't break. And my husband beside me in bed keeps yelling, 'I don't give a damn how you did it before. I'm the commander around here now.'

KING OF THE BARBERS

Sometimes, when he didn't comb his hair, it would fall forward. Down to his nose, like a blindfold. A last wish? the firing squad commander would ask him in a deep baritone. A cigarette maybe? And he'd refuse cavalierly. Fire! the firing squad commander would order. The bullets would hit him and he'd fall. First to his knees, then onto his stomach, the carpet fibers tickling the edges of his nostrils. Long live the Revolution.

He had beautiful hair, very beautiful hair. He'd always known that. And if, let's say, there was some chance he might forget it, that the knowledge might disappear suddenly and be gone forever, it wouldn't be for long. Because his mother would be right there reminding him. She reminded him every night. When he was already in bed, eyes closed, she'd come in carrying his blanket. Cotton in summer, wool in winter. She always came to tuck him in and remind him. Hair like his father's, she'd say, not like Mom's thin, straw hair. Thick straight hair flowing to his shoulders. Like his father's. His father went away and left Mom alone. But Mom isn't alone, Mom has him. Mom runs her soft hand through his hair, surprised every time that there are no knots. And Mom plants wets kisses on his eyes, sometimes even on his mouth.

He didn't remember what his father looked like. He couldn't have remembered. He'd been a bald, premature baby less than a month old during the Sinai Campaign. You can't remember anything from when you're that age. Then his father died, and overnight, he grew a glorious mane of hair, that's what his mother says. After the funeral, they gave her Valium and she fell asleep, and the next morning his head was covered with hair. It was so strange, almost supernatural. The nurses themselves said they'd never seen anything like it.

There wasn't a single picture of his father in the house. That night, before she took the Valium, she burned them all. She said she didn't want the baby either. But she didn't mean that for a minute: after all, when she got up in the morning, the first thing she did when she opened her eyes was run over to see him and his new mane of hair through the glass wall.

Saul was repulsive. He was repulsive, stank of garlic, and his left shoe was black and huge, the right one regular size. Mom said it was a birth defect, his feet weren't the same length. He never said it, but he thought Saul was one big birth defect. With those huge glasses and the way he hugged his mother so close, like an overgrown bear hugging a jar of honey. One big birth defect, nothing about him was right, even his hair was fake. And Mom slept with that beast. She still came to tuck him in at night. Wool in winter, cotton in summer. Ran her soft hand through his hair. Thick, flowing hair, as smooth and straight as his father's. A dry kiss on the forehead, then back to the beast.

One morning, the door was open and he saw Saul lying in bed on his stomach, a round drool stain on the sheet near his mouth and an enormous bald patch in the middle of his head. Most of his hair was on the little table near the door. Tossed under the table were his shoes, the big one crushing the small one. The room looked so weird with that clump of hair lying motionless on the table, like a corpse, and that peculiar bald patch in the middle of his head that could appear and disappear in an instant.

On his way to school, he stopped at a store window and looked at the boy facing him. A boy with thick lips, sunken cheeks and his father's hair. Who knows? He could believe anything about his mother. What with the pictures she burned and saying she didn't want him – maybe she'd done that too and the Valium stopped her later. Maybe his father was lying in his grave, bald, and he was walking around with his father's hair on his head just so Mom would be happy. He tried to take off the toupee with one hard pull. The pain in his scalp was sharp. Holding a clump in his left hand, he examined the ripped-out hairs thoroughly. The base of each hair was white and straight. He smelled them. They smelled of glue. He looked in the store window again. His hair looked exactly like it did before, maybe a little messier. No bald patch, no nothing, most of the hair had stayed on his head. Except that there were letters written above it. He read them slowly: K-i-n-g o-f t-h-e B-a-r-b-e-r-s.

The King of the Barbers had a high chair, a mirror the size of a wall and a frantic electric razor. When you plugged it in, it made noises like a dog does a second before it attacks. The barber told wonderful stories while he was cutting his hair, about Africans with braids and bald men who come in for a haircut every week. And while he talked, he clicked his scissors like they were castanets, circling the chair from every direction. When he was finished, the King asked if he could pick up his hair from the floor and save it as a keepsake. The King had been in the profession for forty years, but he'd never seen such beautiful hair. He said yes right away and kept sitting there, looking at the mirror in front of him. From where he sat, he could see a bald boy on a high chair, and a king on all fours next to him, collecting cut-off hair with his hands.

ABRAM CADABRAM

At five o'clock, two guys from the Bailiff's Office showed up. One of them, fat and sweaty, checked the stuff in the house and filled out forms. The second leaned on the refrigerator, chewing gum.

'You're really in deep shit, huh?' he said to Abram.

'No,' Abram said, shaking his head, 'not me, buddy. I'm the guarantor.'

'You signed for him? So you are in deep shit,' the indifferent one said and opened the refrigerator door. 'Can I?' he asked, pointing to an open bottle of Coke.

'Take it,' Abram said. 'Take it. And there's some

fruit in the drawer on the bottom. If you eat some, it'll be lighter when you carry it down.'

'Hey, I never thought of that,' the indifferent one said and drank straight from the plastic bottle. 'It's flat,' he said, disappointed. 'Kaufman,' he said to the fat guy who'd just walked into the kitchen. 'Want some Coke?'

'Come on, Nissim, stop with the Coke,' the fat guy said angrily. 'Can't you see I'm working?'

'So forget it,' Nissim said and took another swig.

The fat guy went over to Abram and said, 'Say, how many inches is the screen?'

'The screen? What screen?' Abram asked, confused.

'The screen, the TV screen, the one in the carton in the bedroom,' the fat guy said impatiently.

'The TV? Twenty-two inch. But don't touch it, it's not mine, it's a present for my mother. She's sixty next week, on the fifteenth.'

'You bought it?' the fat guy asked.

'Yes, I did, but . . .'

'Pal,' the fat guy said, patting Abram on the shoulder with his sweaty hand, 'when you can't pay your bills, you don't buy presents.'

The fat guy walked out of the kitchen. The other guy gave Abram a sad look. 'It's really insulting not to bring your mother a present, especially for her sixtieth birthday,' he said in his monotone.

Abram didn't answer.

'You're in deep shit, aren't you,' the indifferent one said after a few minutes of silence.

The fat guy came back into the kitchen and said, 'Hey, pal, come here for a minute.'

Abram followed him to the balcony, where the fat guy stopped next to a big wooden trunk. 'What's this?' the fat guy asked.

'It's my magic trunk,' Abram said.

'Magic trunk,' the fat guy said, narrowing his eyes in suspicion. 'What do you mean, magic trunk?'

'I'm a magician,' Abram said, 'and that's where I keep my equipment.'

'How about that!' the indifferent guy said, perking up. He'd followed them to the balcony. 'The whole time I was thinking you look familiar and I don't know from where. You're Abram Cadabram, that magician who appears on the kids' programs with that curly-haired guy and his dog. Every week you teach them how to do a new trick, right? My kid's crazy about you. All day long, he . . .'

'Is this stuff worth a lot of money?' the fat guy interrupted.

'It's worth a lot to me, more than money,' Abram

said. 'But for someone else . . .' he added with a shrug.

'I'll be the one to decide that,' the fat guy said. 'Open it.'

Abram opened the carton and started removing all kinds of things. Kerchiefs, handkerchiefs, wands, jars and wooden boxes.

'What's that?' the fat guy asked, pointing to a medium-sized wooden box with a picture of a fire-breathing dragon carved on the cover.

'I'll show you,' Abram said, grinning at the fat guy. 'It's magic,' he whispered, wiping the dust off his black top hat and putting it on his head. 'Magic from Magic Land.' Cadabram went over to the clock radio on the cabinet, unplugged it and put it in the box. 'Hocus-pocus,' he said and tapped the box twice with a wand he'd taken out of the carton. He opened the box again. It was empty. Nissim whistled admiringly.

'Get that clock back right now! And I mean right now, do you hear me?' the fat guy yelled, waving one of his forms at Abram. 'I already wrote you a receipt for it.'

Cadabram smiled, and when he opened the box again, there was a black cape in it. Cadabram took it and went to the bedroom.

'Don't piss me off, you hear? Put that clock back right now!' the fat guy ordered, following him out.

Cadabram spread the cape on the carton that held the TV he'd bought for his mother.

'What do you think you're doing?' the fat guy asked angrily. Cadabram looked him right in the eye and whispered, 'Allakazam, allakazoom,' and whisked the cape off the carton. The carton stayed where it was. The fat guy breathed a sigh of relief. With the help of the wand he was holding Cadabram opened the lid of the carton. It was empty. Nissim, peering from behind the fat guy's shoulder, applauded enthusiastically.

'Now you really went too far,' the fat guy said. 'I want you to know, pal, that what you just did is a criminal offense, no different than stealing. Do you hear? I'm going to report it to the police now. Now, do you hear?'

The fat guy walked out and slammed the door behind him.

'That was amazing, absolutely amazing,' Nissim said excitedly, 'but you know, that Kaufman is a bastard, he'll really go to the police.'

'No problem,' Abram said, dragging the TV out of its hiding place under the bed. 'It'll take him at least half an hour to come back, enough time to move it to my parents' place.' Nissim helped Abram lift the TV.

'Thanks,' Abram said.

'Tell your mother happy birthday from me too,

okay? Even though I don't know her.' Abram nodded and walked out of the room.

'Hey, Abram,' Nissim yelled after him when he was almost at the front door. Abram stopped and turned around. Nissim was standing at the end of the hallway wearing the top hat, the wand under his armpit. 'Look what I found,' he said, waving the pack of forms the fat guy had filled out. 'Kaufman forgot to take them.' Nissim crumpled all the forms into a little ball and pushed it into his right fist. 'Allakazam, allakazoom,' he whispered, touching his fist with the wand. Then he opened his clutched fist. The forms had vanished. 'Ta-daa!' Nissim cried, swept the top hat off head and took a bow.

VENUS LITE

The gods were very dignified. When they arrived, everyone wanted to help them: the Jewish Agency, the Ministry of Absorption, the Housing Ministry, everyone. But they didn't want anything. They came with nothing, asked for nothing, worked like Arabs and were satisfied. And that's how Mercury ended up in deliveries, Atlas in furniture moving, and Vulcan in an auto body shop. Venus came to our office. To work the photocopier.

I was going through a shitty time. I didn't know what to do with myself. I was alone, so alone. I desperately wanted to have a great love. Usually, when I'm in a state like that, I take up something new, painting, the guitar, whatever. Then, if I manage to get into it, it makes me feel better and I forget that I don't have anyone in the world, but this time, I knew that no macramé course was going to help. I needed something I could believe in. A great love that would never go away, that would never leave me. My therapist listened with interest and suggested that I buy a dog. I left him.

Venus worked from eight-thirty to six, sometimes even later, photocopying dozens of copies of printed pages and stacking them in neat piles. Even in that position, sweaty and bent over the Xerox, the flashing light inside the machine making her close her eyes, she was still the most beautiful thing I'd ever seen. I wanted to tell her that, but I didn't have the courage. In the end, I wrote it down on a piece of paper and left it on the desk for her. The next morning, the note was waiting for me, along with fifty photocopies.

She didn't know Hebrew very well. She was a goddess, but she earned seven thousand shekels before taxes. I know, because once, when I was in the accounting department, I looked at her paycheck. I wanted to marry her, I wanted to save her. I truly believed that she could save me. I don't know how I did it, but I finally asked her if she wanted to go to a movie with me. The girl that

Paris chose as the most beautiful of all the goddesses smiled the gentlest, shyest smile you can imagine and said yes.

Before I left the house, I looked in the mirror. I had a little pimple on my forehead. The Roman goddess of beauty and I are going to a movie tonight, I said to myself, the Roman goddess of beauty and I are going out on a date. I popped the pimple and wiped the greasy blood with a tissue. Who are you, you pathetic mortal, to want to buy her popcorn, to dare to put your arm around her in the darkness of a movie theater?

After the movie, we went somewhere for a drink. I was hoping she wouldn't talk to me about the plot. I had no idea what had happened on the screen. I'd been looking at her through the whole movie. We talked a little about work and how her family was adjusting in Israel. She liked it here. Sure, she wanted more out of life, and she'd get it, but meanwhile, she definitely liked it here. Oh God, she said, touching my arm, you have no idea how awful it was for us there.

Driving her home, I asked whether she really believed in God. She laughed. If you're asking whether I know that he exists, she said, then the answer is yes. Not just him, lots of other gods. But if you're asking whether I believe in him, then no, definitely not.

We got to her house and she was already opening the car door. I cursed myself for taking the short route. I wanted so much for her to stay with me a little longer. I prayed for a miracle. For the police to stop us, for someone to kidnap us, for something to happen that would leave us together. Already out of the car, she asked me to come up for coffee.

She's sleeping now, next to me, in bed. Lying on her stomach, her head sunk into the pillow. Her lips move slightly, as if she's saying something to herself silently. Her right arm is hugging me, her hand resting on my chest. I try not to breathe more than I have to so the rising and falling of my chest won't wake her. She's beautiful, really beautiful. Perfect. And pretty nice too. But that's it. Tomorrow I'm buying a dog.

THROUGH WALLS

She had this kind of look in her eyes, half disappointment half what-difference-does-it-make. Like someone who finds out he bought skim milk by mistake and doesn't have the energy to take it back. 'It's really nice,' she said, putting the cactus in a corner of the room. Then she said, 'Look, Yoav, I don't know what you have in mind, it's just important to me that you know I'm living here with someone.'

Once, I thought it was terribly important for my girlfriend to be pretty. It was essential for her to be smart and we had to be in love and all that, but I really, really wanted her to be pretty too. I used to read a lot of comic books then. My hero was The Vision. He could fly, walk through walls. His look could kill. The Vision wasn't a person, he was an android. You couldn't tell from looking at him: he had a girlfriend and everything. He was special, didn't look like anyone I'd ever met. He had a red face with a jewel in the middle of his forehead and a green suit. The Vision always wore green, no matter what.

We'd meet at parties sometimes. She'd come with her boyfriend. He looked okay, but ordinary. She didn't look like anyone I'd ever met. When they stood together at a party, dozens of people around them, you knew right away which one of them was the lead and which one was the extra. She deserved more than that, and I knew it. I wanted to shake her, to snatch her right out of there. I didn't understand why I didn't say anything.

The Vision may have been made of synthetic materials, but he had lots of feelings. In one of the comic books, he even cried. It was on the last page, and the caption under it said, 'Even an android can cry.' He was big. He was a giant. He was the leader of the Avengers. Her boyfriend and I once peed next to each other in a university bathroom and his urine came out dark yellow. I wanted to kill him. For myself, but also because he defiled her with that ordinariness of his. I pictured myself drowning him in the toilet bowl, killing him with a death stare. But I didn't do that. I didn't do anything. He shook himself twice, put it in his pants and zipped up. He didn't even flush. When he finished washing his hands, he put them under the dryer. I could have banged his head against the mirror, the sink, the floor, a hundred places. He smiled at me, completely unafraid, and walked out of the bathroom.

I was mad at myself. I felt terrible. I knew that the feeling would never end, like a headache that doesn't go away. I looked in the filthy mirror across from me. I was special, I didn't look like anyone I'd ever met. I wanted to shake myself, to snatch myself right out of there. I knew I deserved more than that. I didn't understand why I didn't say anything.

Ronit got married in August. Her boyfriend became her husband. My parents said that he was a very nice guy, but I knew. He won't go through walls for her. Neither will I. I went through glass once. At a student demonstration. Two policemen threw me through a store window. A few years later, we met on the street. She had a baby. She asked me what the scar was from, then she started to cry. 'God,' she said. 'What they did to your face.' I gave the baby my death stare. It didn't work. But after five seconds, he started crying too. 'God, you used to be so good-looking,' she said, wiping her face with a diaper. She never even noticed that her baby was screaming. Once, I would have gone through walls for her.

THE FLYING SANTINIS

Italo waved his left hand and the annoying drumroll stopped. He took a long breath and closed his eyes. When I saw him standing there like that, poised on the small wooden board in his glittering show costume, almost touching the canvas ceiling of the big top, everything suddenly fell into place. I'd leave home and join the circus! I'd become one of the Flying Santinis, I'd leap through the air like a demon, I'd hang from the trapeze ropes by my teeth!

Italo vaulted through the air two and a half times, and in the middle of the third somersault, grabbed the extended arm of Enrico, the youngest Santini. The crowd jumped to its feet, applauding wildly, and my father snatched my box of popcorn and threw it in the air. Salty snowflakes landed on my head.

Some children have to run away from home at night to join the circus, but I was driven there by my father. He and my mother helped me pack my clothes in a suitcase. 'I'm so proud of you, son,' Dad said and hugged me as I was about to knock on the door of Papa Luigi's trailer.

'Farewell, Ariel-Marcello Santini. And think about me and your mother a little every time you fly high above the circus floor.'

Papa Luigi opened the door wearing his glittering show pants and a striped pajama top. 'I want to join you, Papa Luigi,' I whispered. 'I want to be a Flying Santini.'

Papa Luigi scrutinized my body, felt the muscles of my skinny forearms with interest and finally let me in.

'So many children want to be Flying Santinis,' he said after a few seconds of silence. 'Why do you think *you* should be the one?' I didn't know how to answer so I bit my lower lip and said nothing. 'Are you brave?' Papa Luigi asked. I nodded. Papa Luigi whipped his fist right up to my face. I didn't flinch, didn't even blink. 'Hmm . . .' Papa Luigi said, rubbing his chin. 'And agile?' he asked. 'You do know that the Flying Santinis are famous for their agility, don't you?'

I nodded again, biting down hard on my lower lip. Papa Luigi extended his right hand, put a hundred lira coin in it and signaled me with his graying eyebrows. I managed to grab it before he could close his fist. He nodded in admiration. 'Now only the final test is left,' he said, his voice thundering. 'The flexibility test. You have to touch your shoes without bending your knees.' I relaxed my body, took a long breath and closed my eyes just like Italo, my brother, had done in the show that night. I bent over and reached down. I could see the tips of my fingers a few millimeters from my shoelaces, almost touching. My body was as taut as a rope about to snap, but I didn't give up. Four millimeters separated me from the Santinis. I knew that I had to get past them. Then suddenly I heard it. A deafening sound, like wood and glass breaking together. The noise alarmed my father, who must have been waiting outside in the car, and he came running into the trailer. 'Are you all right?' he asked, trying to help me get up. I couldn't straighten out. Papa Luigi picked me up in his strong arms and we all drove to the hospital.

The X-rays showed a herniated disc between L2 and L3. Holding it up to the light, I could see a sort of black spot, like a drop of coffee, on my transparent spine. Written in ballpoint on the big brown envelope was 'Ariel Fledermaus'. No

Marcello, no Santini – just that crooked, ugly handwriting. 'You could have bent your knees,' Papa Luigi whispered, wiping a tear from my eye. 'You could have bent them a little. I wouldn't have said anything.'

ONE HUNDRED PER CENT

I touch her hands, her face, her hair down below, her shirt. And I say to her, 'Roni, please take it off, for me.' But she won't. So I back down and we do it again, touch each other, completely naked, almost. The tag on her shirt says the material is one hundred per cent cotton, it's supposed to feel good, but it's scratchy. Nothing is one hundred per cent, that's what she always says, just ninety-nine point nine, God willing. Spit three times, she says, then knock on wood three times, now! I hate that shirt. It scratches my face, it doesn't let me feel how hot her body is, whether she's sweating too. And I say it again: 'Roni, please.' My voice, a faint scream like the sound of someone biting himself with a closed mouth. I'm coming, please take it off. She's adamant. She won't.

It's crazy. We've been together six months and I still haven't seen her naked. Six months, and my friends are still telling me not to make any moves on her. Six months of living together and they keep on telling me stories that everybody knows by heart already. How she stood in front of the mirror and tried to cut her breasts off with a kitchen knife because she hated the shape of her body. How she was hospitalized, more than once. And they tell me those stories about her as if she were a stranger, while they're drinking our coffee from our mugs. They tell me not to get involved with her when we're already madly in love. I could kill them for that, but I don't say anything. At most, I ask them to be quiet and hate them silently. What can they tell me about her that I don't already know? What can they say that would make me love her even one drop less?

I try to explain it to her. That it doesn't matter. That what we have is so strong that nothing can destroy it, I spit three times, then knock on wood three times, like she wants me to. That I know, that I've already been told, I know what's there and I couldn't care less. But it doesn't help, nothing helps with her. She's adamant. The furthest we ever got was after a bottle of chianti at a New Year's party, and even then, it was only one button.

After she gets the test results, she calls her girlfriend, who did it once, to find out what the procedure is. She doesn't want an abortion, I can feel that. I don't want one either. I tell her that. I get down on my knees in a dramatic pose and ask her to marry me: 'Come on, babe,' I say in my most Dean Martin voice. 'Let's ring-a-ding-ding.' She laughs; she says no. She asks if it's because she's pregnant, but she knows it isn't. Five minutes later, she says okay, but on the condition that if it's a boy, we call him Yotam. We shake on it. I try to get up, but my legs have fallen asleep.

That night, we get into bed. We kiss. We undress. Only the shirt stays on. She pushes me away. She unbuttons a button. And another one, slowly, like a stripper, one hand holding the lapel closed, the other unbuttoning another button. After she goes through all of them, she looks at me, looks deeply into my eyes. I'm breathing heavily now. She lets the shirt fall open. And I see, I see what's under it. Nothing can destroy what we have, nothing, that's what I always said. God, how could I have been so stupid.

THE GIRL ON THE

REFRIGERATOR

Alone

He told her that he once had a girlfriend who liked to be alone. And that was very
sad, because they were a couple, and couple, by
definition, means together. But mostly she
preferred to be alone. So once he asked her, 'Why?
Is it something in me?' And she said, 'No, it has
nothing to do with you, it's something in me, from
my childhood.' He didn't really get it, the
childhood thing, so to understand it a tiny bit
better, he tried to find something similar in his

own childhood, but he couldn't find anything. The more he thought about it, the more his childhood seemed like a hole in someone else's tooth – unhealthy, but not too annoying, at least not to him. And that girl, who liked to be alone, kept hiding from him, and all because of her childhood. It really pissed him off. Finally, he told her, 'Either you explain it to me, or we stop being a couple.' She said okay, and they stopped being a couple.

Ogette is Sympathetic

'That's very sad,' Ogette said. 'Sad and at the same time, moving.' 'Thanks,' Nahum said and took a sip of his juice. Ogette saw that he was crying a little and she didn't want to upset him, but in the end, she couldn't resist, and she asked, 'So to this day you don't know what it was in her childhood that made her leave you?' 'She didn't leave me,' Nahum corrected her. 'We broke up.' 'Whatever you say,' Ogette said. 'It's not "whatever I say",' Nahum insisted. 'It's my life. For me, at least, those details are important.' 'And to this day, you don't know what event in her childhood started all this?' Ogette continued. 'It wasn't an event that started all this,' Nahum corrected her again. 'It was you.' And after a short silence, he added, 'Yes, something to do with the refrigerator.'

Not Nahum's

When Nahum's girlfriend was little, her parents had no patience with her because she was little and full of energy, and they were already old and worn-out. Nahum's girlfriend tried to play with them, talk to them, but that only annoyed them more. They didn't have the strength. They didn't even have enough strength to tell her to shut her mouth. So instead, they used to hoist her up, sit her on the refrigerator and go to work. Or wherever they had to go. The refrigerator was very high, and Nahum's girlfriend couldn't get down. And so it happened that she spent most of her childhood on top of the refrigerator. It was a very happy childhood. While other people had the crap beaten out of them by their big brothers, Nahum's girlfriend sat on the edge of the refrigerator, sang to herself and drew little pictures in the layer of dust that had collected there. The view from up there was very beautiful, and her bottom was nice and warm. Now that she was older, she missed that time, that alone time, very much. Nahum understood how sad it made her, and once he even tried to fuck her on top of the refrigerator, but that didn't work. 'That's an awfully beautiful story,' Ogette whispered, brushing Nahum's hand with hers. 'Yes,' Nahum mumbled, pulling his arm back. 'An awfully beautiful story, but not mine.'

ATONEMENT

Right to his face she said it, on the front steps of the synagogue. As soon as they'd walked out, even before he'd had a chance to put the yarmulke back in his pocket. She made him let go of her hand and told him that he was an animal, that he'd better never dare talk to her that way again, dragging her out like she was some piece of goods. And she said it out loud too, people could hear it. People who worked with him, even the rabbi, but that didn't stop her from raising her voice. He should've slapped her right then and there, should've shoved her right down the stairs. But, like an idiot, he waited till they got home. And then, when he beat her, she seemed so taken aback. Like a dog that you hit for shitting on the carpet when so much time has passed that the shit is all dry. He kept at it, smacking her across the face, and she shouted, 'Menachem, Menachem!' as if the person beating her was some stranger and she was crying out for him to come and save her. 'Menachem, Menachem!' she cringed in the corner. 'Menachem, Menachem!' and he gave her a kick in the ribs.

As he moved away from her to light a cigarette, he noticed the spot of blood on his synagogue shoes, and he looked at her again and saw a red crescent on the dress he'd bought her for the holidays. The crescent kept growing fuller. She must have been bleeding from the nose. He pulled up a dining-room chair and sat down with his back to her, facing the electric clock. Behind him he could hear her crying. He could hear the moans as she kept trying to get back on her feet, the thump as she slipped back into her corner. The hands of the electric clock were moving at an alarming speed, and he loosened his belt, gave up the back of the chair and tilted his body forward.

'I'm sorry,' he heard her whimper from the corner. 'I'm sorry, Menachem. I didn't mean it, really, forgive me.' And he forgave her and so did God, and the timing was truly perfect, with only thirty seconds to go till it's too late to offer forgiveness.

GAZA BLUES

Weismann had a rasping dry cough, the hack of a tubercular, and the whole way there he kept coughing, and spitting into tissues.

'It's the cigarettes,' he said apologetically. 'They're just killing me.' When we reached the Erez roadblock, we parked the car at the gas station. There was a taxi waiting for us there, with a local license plate. 'Did you remember to bring the forms?' Weismann asked and spat a yellow gob on the sidewalk. I nodded. 'How about the powers of attorney?' Weismann kept at it. I said yes, those too.

We didn't have to tell the driver anything. He knew to take us straight to Fadid's office. It was late

May already, but the streets were flooded. Must be some problem with the plumbing. 'Shitty road,' the driver complained. 'Every three week, tires finish.' I figured he must be setting the stage to hike the price.

We walked into Fadid's office, and he shook our hands. 'Let me introduce you,' Weismann said. 'This is Niv, a junior clerk in our firm. He's here to learn.' 'Keep your eyes open, Niv,' Fadid turned to me and spoke in perfect Hebrew. 'Keep your eyes open wide and look around you. There's a lot to learn here.' Fadid led us into his office. 'You sit here,' he told Weismann, pointing to the leather chair behind the desk. 'And this,' he pointed to a small wooden stool in the corner, 'this is for the interpreter. I'll be back at two. Make yourselves at home.' I sat down on the leather couch in the office and laid out the forms in five separate piles on the low table beside me. Meanwhile, the interpreter arrived. 'There are four cases,' he said. His name was Mas'oud or something. 'Two eye, two leg, one ball.' From the way Weismann had described it, it wouldn't take more than twenty minutes to get the forms signed for each case plus an interview, which meant that in an hour and a half tops we'd be heading back. Weismann asked them the usual questions through the interpreter and chain-smoked. I had them sign the medical secrecy waivers and powers of attorney and explained to each of them through the interpreter that if they won we'd take a cut that varies from fifteen to twenty per cent. One of them, a half-blind woman, signed with her thumb, like in the movies. The guy who got it in the balls asked in Hebrew, when I'd finished explaining, if the Security Service guy who kicked his balls in would wind up in jail if we won. 'I know his name and I don't afraid say it in court,' he said. 'Steve, *in'al abu*, that was his name.' The interpreter told him off in Arabic for speaking in Hebrew. 'If you want to talk with them yourself,' he said, 'you don't need me. I can wait outside.' I know a little Arabic. Took it in high school.

An hour and ten minutes later we were already back in the taxi, and on our way to the Erez roadblock. Fadid had invited us for lunch, but Weismann explained that we were in a hurry. Weismann didn't stop coughing and spitting into his tissues the whole way back. 'Is no good, Mister,' the driver told him. 'You should go to doctor. My sister husband he doctor. Live near here.' 'No thanks, I'm okay. I'm used to it,' Weismann tried to smile at him. 'It's all on account of the cigarettes. They're doing me in, slowly but surely.'

We hardly spoke the whole way home. I was thinking about my 5 o'clock basketball practice. 'In three of the cases, we stand a chance,' Weismann said. 'Except the one with the balls. For the whole three years he spent in jail after the interrogation there's no mention of his injury. Go prove that they did it to him three and a half years ago.' 'But you're taking him on anyway?' I asked. 'Yeah,' Weismann mumbled. 'I didn't say I wouldn't take him on. I just said we don't stand a chance.' He kept fiddling with the radio dial, trying to pick up something, but all he got was static. After that he tried humming something, but a few seconds later he got bored, lit up and started coughing again. Then he asked me once more if I'd remembered to have them sign everything. I said I had. 'You know what.' He turned to me suddenly. 'I should have been born black. Every time I come out of there I tell myself: "Weismann, you should have been born black." Not here, somewhere far away, like New Orleans maybe.' He opened the car window and flicked out the cigarette. 'Billy, that's what my name should have been. Billy Whiteman, that's a good name for a singer.' He cleared his throat as though he were about to start singing, but as soon as he inhaled he started coughing and wheezing. 'See this?' he said when he was finished, and showed me the used tissue up close, the one he'd coughed into. 'It's something I made up all by myself. Strong stuff, eh? "Billy Whiteman and the Dismals", that's what they'd call my band. We'd sing nothing but blues.'

AN EXCLUSIVE

I was knocking down a wall.

All women reporters are whores and I was knocking down a wall. It was already something like four months after she left. At first, I thought all that renovating would calm me down, but all it did was just upset me more. The wall I was knocking down was the one between the living room and the bedroom. So that the balcony was always behind me. But I remembered. You don't have to see to remember. I remembered how we used to sit there all night.

'Look,' she said to me, 'a falling star. We have to make a wish now. Come on,' she said, kissing me on the neck, 'wish for something.' 'Okay,' I said, giving in, 'I'm wishing.' 'What did you wish?' she asked, giving me a hug. 'Tell me, please, tell me.' 'That it'll always be like this, like it is now.' I ran my hand over her hair. 'A breeze. The two of us together on the balcony.' 'No,' she said, pushing me away, 'that's not a good wish. Wish for something else, something just for you.' 'Okay, okay,' I said with a laugh, 'just stop pushing. An FZR 1000. I wish for a Yamaha FZR 1000.' 'A motorcycle?' She looked at me, shocked. 'You get a wish and you ask for a motorcycle?' 'Yes,' I said. 'What did you wish for?' 'I'm not telling,' she said, hiding her face in my sweater. 'If you tell, it never comes true.'

But if you don't tell, maybe it does. Two months later, she moved to Tel Aviv to work on a daily paper, not just the local rag. She didn't say a word to me, just disappeared. Her parents wouldn't give me her address. They said she asked them to tell me she didn't want to talk to me. 'Why not?' I asked her father. 'Did I hurt her feelings? Did I do something to her?' 'I don't know,' he said, shrugging. 'That's what she told me to say.' 'Tell me, Mr Brosh,' I said, getting angry, 'you think it's normal that your daughter and I have been going out together for two years, and all of a sudden, just like that, for no reason, she doesn't want to talk to me? You don't think I deserve an explanation?' 'That's not fair, Eli,' her father said, leaning on the door handle. The whole conversation was taking place at the door to their apartment. 'It really isn't fair,' he said, running his free hand over his bald head. 'I'm not the one who left you, you know. I never did anything bad to you, right? I don't deserve for you to be talking to me in that tone.' He was right. Simple as that. I said I was sorry and left. Suddenly, he looked so forlorn. After that, I tried to get her through the paper. But they wouldn't give me her home number, and she was never at the office. So I left her a message, I left a thousand messages, but she didn't call. A few months later, I decided to renovate.

People were screaming. Between one blow and another on the wall, I suddenly realized that people were screaming on the street, not far from my house. I went outside. Near the intersection, thirty meters from me, two people were lying on the road, and a woman was running towards me, yelling, and a man in a green woolen hat was chasing her. About ten meters away from me, he caught up with her and grabbed her by the hair. Suddenly, I saw the tip of a knife sticking out of the front of her neck. And blood, a ton of blood. She fell to her knees, the man pulled his arm back and the blade just disappeared. She was lying on the sidewalk now. And the guy with the knife was looking at me, moving slightly towards me, but slowly. I wanted to run away, but my feet just wouldn't move. He kept coming closer, taking small, hesitant steps as if we were kids playing tag. And the whole time, I kept saying to myself, something's not right here. Why's he walking so slowly? I mean, he ran after that woman like a madman. Here I am in my slippers and he's holding a knife twenty centimeters long. What's he afraid of? Why doesn't he come and stab me? And then I saw him step off the sidewalk onto the road, trying to walk around me very, very slowly. I watched him, half aware of the sledgehammer in my hand, a five-kilo sledgehammer. I took a step towards him and whacked him on the head with it.

He wasn't moving. I sat down on the sidewalk. The guy from the grocery came over to me with a Coke. I put my hand in the pocket of my sweat pants to pay him. He grabbed it and wouldn't let me take out the money. 'Forget it,' he said, 'it's on me.' 'Come on, Gaby,' I said, 'let me pay.' But he insisted and wouldn't let go of my hand. 'So put it on my bill,' I said, backing down. I was thirsty and wanted to settle the whole thing before I started drinking, while I was still in a bargaining position. 'Okay, okay,' he said, 'I'll put it on your bill.'

The photographers got there first, even before the police. On motorcycles, two on a 600F and one on a Harley. With their long hair and tattoos, they

177

looked just like Hell's Angels. 'Hold the hammer like this, would you, like you're threatening him, just for a picture?' the guy with the Harley asked me. I said no. 'Are you sure?' he asked, still trying. 'Visually speaking, it would be much stronger.' After that, the police came, then the newspaper reporters. All reporters are whores.

They came from all the papers. I wouldn't talk to them. They came from TV and from radio too. I didn't even tell them no, I just raised my hand and turned away. The TV people went over to Gaby and almost everybody else followed them, except the guy from the *Jerusalem Post*, who kept pestering me. 'Hey, you, four-eyes,' I yelled to one of the newspaper reporters who was trying to push his tape recorder down a police detective's throat. 'Come here.' The guy with the glasses left the detective in the middle of a sentence and came over to me. 'You're from *Haaretz*?' I asked. 'Yeah, I am,' he said excitedly, trying to turn on the tape recorder. 'How come you'll talk to him and not me?' the nudnik from the *Jerusalem Post* said, insulted. 'Because I feel like it, okay?' I was out of patience. 'Because your paper's shit. What difference does it make why? Would you please piss off?' I gestured for the guy with the glasses to walk over to the side with me, but the *Jerusalem Post* guy was like glue. 'It's because of their circulation,' he said in a hurt voice. 'It's just because of their circulation, you egomaniac. You wanna play it big time, eh? So all your pals see what a hero you are. You macho shit, you murderer, you make me sick.' He spat and left. 'Okay,' the *Haaretz* guy said. 'First of all I want to ask you . . .' 'First of all, you listen,' I said. I took the tape recorder out of his hand and pressed stop. 'Go to your editor now and tell him I'm ready to do an exclusive interview for you. Exclusive, you hear? I won't talk to TV, or radio or my own grandmother. But only if . . .' 'We don't pay people we interview,' the guy with the glasses interrupted me. 'It's a principle with us. We don't pay people we interview.' 'Listen to me for a second, you moron,' I said, pissed off. 'I don't want any money from you. I just want to decide who interviews me, got that? Tell him I'm ready to be interviewed, but only by Dafna Brosh. 'Brosh,' the guy with the glasses said, scratching his head, 'that new girl? But she's not sharp.' 'Sharp or not, tell him she's the only one I'll do an interview with.' 'Excuse me,' Glasses said, 'I know this has nothing to do with it, but did you ever by chance read my article on the dairy cartel?' 'Dafna Brosh,' I said again, and left him there.

To get to my apartment now, I had to walk through a huge circle of people who were standing around Gaby. They were shouting and screaming, and he was standing there in the middle, waving his hands, looking like he was having a pretty good time. Two soldiers from the army radio station with microphones in their hands had come a little late and were trying to push their way into the circle, but couldn't. One of them, the taller one, got an elbow in his face from the cameraman of one of the foreign networks. He started bleeding from the nose, his eyes swelled up and tears just sprayed out of them. I decided to head in the other direction and get to my building through a parallel street, even though it would take longer. 'Egomaniac!' the *Jerusalem Post* guy yelled behind me.

She came. I knew she would. Wearing a black mini-shirt, her hair in a blunt cut. 'Want some coffee?' I asked, trying to sound calm. 'Should I put the kettle on?' She shook her head, sat down at the table and took a mini-tape recorder out of her bag. There were large pieces of plaster scattered all over the table. With the half-knocked-down wall in the middle of the room, the place looked like it had been bombed. 'Are you sure?' I asked. 'I'll go put the kettle on.' The head-shaking got sharper, more nervous. 'An interview,' she said, the words coming out of her throat as if she were choking, 'I came for an interview.' She put the tape recorder on the table.

Interview (A)

– *Why?*

– *Am I allowed to ask exactly why you left me?*

– *Don't shrug your shoulders. Answer me. The least I deserve is an answer.*

I don't want to hurt you. Definitely not now. There's no point in it.

– *Hurt me, damn you, hurt me. It can't be worse than what you already did.*

Because you're a nobody, okay? Because you're a nobody. Because you don't want anything. Nothing. Don't want to know anything, don't want to succeed at anything, don't want to be anything. Just to sit on your ass and say how good we have it together. Good is doing things, trying to achieve something, but you? You don't even know how to dream. The only thing you're capable of doing is sitting on that balcony with your arms around me, saying, 'I love, I love, I love.' I'm not a teddy bear or a Goldilocks doll, you know. And unlike you, I have dreams a tiny bit bigger than sleeping late.

– *Do you still love me?*

– *Do you love me a little?*

– *Did you ever love me?*

– *Enough, don't cry. I'm stopping. I stopped. Look. You can ask your questions now.*

Interview (B)

– *What were you doing on the street at the time of the incident?*

Nothing.

– *Were you on your way somewhere?*

No. I wasn't on my way anywhere. I just heard yelling, so I went outside to see.

– *And the hammer?*

I whacked him on the head with it. God, when I try to remember that, it seems so far away, like in a movie.

– *Yes, but why did you have a hammer in your hand?*

Because of the renovations. I'm knocking down the wall between the living room and the bedroom.

– *Did you get a good look at him before it happened? Could you see his face?*

Yes, it was a little chubby. He had these big brown eyes, like yours. And his mouth was slightly twisted, like something was wrong. Like he was constipated, in pain.

– *What passed through your mind when you whacked him with the hammer?*

Nothing.

– *Don't say nothing. You thought something.*

Nothing. Absolutely nothing.

– *I talked to Gaby from the grocery. He told me that the Arab didn't get anywhere near you, that he was afraid*

1

when he saw you with the hammer, that he tried to walk around you, to get away. But you still smashed his skull. You could've waited, you know, you could've just stood there and he would've gone away. At least, that's what the Eli I knew would've done.

I was thinking about you.

We heard the sound of a motorcycle outside. 'That's the photographer,' she said. 'His name's Eli too.' 'What kind of motorcycle does he have?' I asked. 'Since when do I know anything about motorcycles?' she said, laughing. 'Just asking,' I said. 'I thought you might know.' 'An FZR 1000,' she answered, 'he has a Yamaha FZR 1000, like you wished for.' 'You know, if I hadn't told you then, I'd have one too.' 'I know,' she said, forcing a smile. 'I'm sorry.'

MAGICIANS SCHOOL

I'll never forget the graduation ceremony at Magicians High School. The principal called the ten top students to the stage and each one did a trick. Eliav Morgenstein glided above the audience of parents like a bird, Elad Livnat turned cornflakes into sawdust and Abigail Fitzsimmons, my girlfriend at the time, built a bridge of matches between the stage and the VIP section as a symbol of the connection between the future generation of magicians and the tradition of past magicians. I was so proud of her for that. Altogether, it was a special evening. At the end, we all received a diploma and a pin. Written on the pin was, 'I Can Do Anything' and the date of our graduation.

Inscribed in gold letters on the back of the pin was the slogan of the International Magicians Association: 'The Sky's the Limit'. I really love that slogan. Every morning of those four years of school I'd stop my bike in front of the gates to Magicians University and read it in huge letters fastened onto marble. There were a lot of beggars at the gate who always pestered passers-by for money and things like that. But I didn't care. I'd spend all the time I had before my first class standing there and repeating that slogan over and over again in my mind. It gave me a lot of strength.

The Magicians University accepted me right into the Master's program, which was based mainly on independent work. We'd sit in front of the 'I-Can-Do-Anything' computers and scroll down the menus searching for new magic to specialize in. Most of the indexes were alphabetized, jam-packed with tricks jostling for position. 'Exhaling Fire', 'Expanding Breasts (for women only)', 'Extracting Water from a Stone' – they were all there. All you had to do was go over the list and choose.

No one came to the graduation ceremony to see me receive my Master's degree. Abigail and I had just split up and both my parents had died in a plane crash two months earlier. My father was the one who'd pushed me towards magic from the time I was a kid. I was very sorry he couldn't see me there on the stage. At the ceremony, all the graduates got to demonstrate something from their theses. Amicam Shneidman, who was undoubtedly the great Israeli hope in the field of classical magic, showed how he turned staplers into animals, Mahmud al-Mi'ari shrank himself into miniature size and talked to things that didn't exist. I killed a cow. After the ceremony, I was thinking about something else as I was pulling out of the parking lot and boom! After it died, it turned back into a stapler.

Master's degree in hand, I went to America. Magicians are more highly appreciated there than in Israel, and I had no one left here anyway. I traveled around the country a lot, always to new places. Magicians don't work – after all, performing magic isn't a profession – they just go from place to place and do what they want. I fucked a lot. I was really scoring then and had a girl in every city. In other countries, there's a special aura around magicians, something like what Air Force pilots have in Israel, and anyway, American girls don't need a special reason to fall into bed with a guy.

I didn't love any of them except Marcy. I met her in New York, at a McDonald's, where she was a cashier. Two days later, we moved in together and she quit her job. We spent our days walking around the city, and when our money ran out, I'd make us some bills from empty soft drink cans. We were happy. I never thought for a minute that it would ever end. Then one day we were walking down into the subway and passed a man who'd had both his legs amputated. He was sitting in a corner with an empty cup next to him. Marcy asked me to help him, so I picked a can of Diet Coke off the floor and turned it into a hundred-dollar bill. I put it into his cup. The double amputee looked very happy. He waved the bill around in one hand and slapped his left stump enthusiastically with the other. Right then our train pulled into the station, but Marcy refused to get on. She said it wasn't enough. I looked around for more empty cans but couldn't find any. Marcy said that wasn't it, it wasn't money. She wanted me to give him his legs back. I didn't know what to tell her; I wasn't too good when it came to amputees. If it had been a disease or a birth defect, I could've improvised, but when it came to making stumps grow, I was clueless. The amputee and I looked at each other, and he said, 'Hey, no problem. You gave me a hundred, man.' I felt the same way, but Marcy was really boiling. 'Maybe there's still something else I can do for you?' I asked him, mainly so Marcy would calm down. 'Do for me?' he said with a laugh. 'I love that pin on your jacket.' So I gave it to him. I wasn't too thrilled about the idea, but I didn't want to make

Marcy even madder, so I gave him the pin. He stuck it on his filthy shirt. 'Look at me,' he said, laughing. 'I can do anything, man. I'm a crazy mother fucker who can do anything.'

On our way home, Marcy cried and said she hated me, she was going back to work with hamburgers and she never wanted to see me again. At first, I thought it was just a small blow-up, that it would pass after another stop or two and we'd hug again and make up. I was wrong. She got off at Union Square, the doors closed behind her and I never saw her again. I rode to the last stop, picking cans and bottles off the floor and turning them into money. At the exit to the street, I had more than six hundred dollars. It was late already, after two. I started walking back towards Manhattan, looking for an all-night liquor store.

ANTS

I cut off the heads with a knife, one by one, to make sure it comes out even. Then I pile them high in front of the opening of the nest, and I wait. One ant is coming back to the nest now, with a little breadcrumb. It climbs onto the pile, without the slightest idea of what's waiting for it. I light a match and the ant starts to burn.

Mom says I have to study on my own now that I'm not in school any more. But Dad told me more than once that all you learn in school is lies and bullshit. And I'm not too keen on studying lies and bullshit on my own, so I take care of the ants instead.

Mom and Dad hardly ever talk to each other since I stopped going to school. Mom blames Dad for what happened. 'They warned me about you,' I heard her yell at him once. 'They told me not to marry you. Look at you. You sleep till noon every day, you don't work, you walk around the house naked. The boy is ashamed of you. I hope you realize that. That's why he's outside all the time.'

I'm not ashamed or anything like that. I'm just a little busy now. I started a training program for the ants. It works great. I give an order – and they carry it out right away, no hesitation, in half a second.

I'm like God to them. I can do whatever I want to them, and they know it. If I feel like it, their nest will be bursting with food. If they make me mad, they'll end up smeared on the bottom of my sandal.

Mom left the house, took me with her and went to live with Robin Schweig, but I ran away back home. I have a plan now. A plan of revenge that will give my dad his honor back. It's very simple. I just have to stick to the training plan.

Two ants are a crumb, ten are a leaf from an olive tree, thirty billion are a whole school rising in the air. 'Put us down,' Mensch yells at them. 'I order you to put us down immediately.' But the ants piss on him. They only take orders from me. The kids are jumping out of the classroom windows now, and with each one that jumps, the building gets lighter, and the ants can move faster. In less than five minutes, they're running.

I go back home now, a hero. Not only do the ants admire me, the kids in my class do too. There's no more school, no one to laugh at Dad. Now everything's going to be just like it was before. I want to tell Dad, but he's not home. I check the rooms one by one. He's not in the living room or the bedroom. Maybe he's already heard it's all over, I think, and he's back at work. But he isn't; I see him from the kitchen window, in the yard, naked, down on all fours next to the ants' nest.

FREEZE!

Suddenly, I could do it. I'd say 'Freeze!' and everyone would freeze, just like that, in the middle of the street. Cars, bicycles, even those little motor scooters delivery boys use would stop in their tracks. And I'd walk past them looking for the prettiest girls. I'd tell them to drop their shopping bags or I'd take them off a bus, bring them home and fuck their brains out. It was great, just fantastic. 'Freeze!' 'Come here!' 'Lie down on the bed!' And after that, wham-bam. The girls I had were great-looking, centerfold material. I felt awesome. I felt like a king. Until my mother started mixing in.

She told me she wasn't completely happy with the whole business. I told her there was no reason not to be happy. I tell the girls to come and they come. I don't rape them or anything. And my mother said, 'No, no. God forbid. It's just that there's something very impersonal about it. Unemotional. I don't know how to explain it, but I have this gut feeling that you don't really connect with them.' So I told my mother that she could keep her gut feelings to herself. I told her that she could do what she wants and I'd do what I want. I told her 'Freeze!' and left her like that in the middle of Reiness Street in the pouring rain. I was really pissed at her for sticking her nose in my business.

Since then, it hasn't been the same. What she said suddenly bothered me, that I don't connect. I kept fucking the girls, but I didn't really feel connected. Everything was ruined. At first I thought it was the sounds. So I'd say to the girls, 'Make sounds.' And they'd make all kinds of sounds: Mickey Mouse, jackhammers, political impersonations. It was a nightmare, a real nightmare. I had to demonstrate the actual words I wanted them to say. 'Aaaah, aaaah', 'That's so good', 'Harder'. That kind of stuff. And they'd repeat them when we were fucking, but always in my intonation. 'Oh, oh, please don't stop. I'm coming,' they'd say as they lay there on their backs, eyes glazed. I knew they were lying and it made me so mad I could've strangled them. 'If you don't mean it, don't say it.' I'd yell that a few times, but I couldn't keep doing it. It was depressing, so depressing.

But I finally understood what was screwing it all up. My problem was that I insisted on being too specific. At some point, I figured that out and then I started telling them more general things like, 'Act like you're really enjoying it,' and when the feeling they were faking it started to bother me, I'd just say, 'Enjoy it.' It was terrific, absolutely terrific. They'd scream. They'd dig their nails into my back. They'd say, 'You're the best.' Can you picture it? Models, air hostesses, weather girls, in my bed, telling me I'm great.

Except that then, knowing they were there just because I told them to be started to bother me. It hit me out of the blue, like a blast to my brain. I was walking past Reiness Street, at the corner of Gordon. My mother was still standing there with that apologetic look on her face exactly where I left her, and I suddenly understood: this wasn't the real thing, it never would be. Because none of those girls really appreciates me. None of them wants me because of what I really am. And if they're not with me because of what I am, then it just isn't worth a damn. Right then, I decided to stop and to hit on girls the regular way. It was a flop, a fiasco, just a terrible time. Girls I used to fuck in the middle of the street while they were leaning on mailboxes suddenly refused to give me their numbers. They started saying things to me like my breath stinks or I don't turn them on or they have a boyfriend. It was grim, absolutely grim. But I wanted a real relationship so badly that even though the temptation to go back to fucking like I used to was enormous, I didn't give in.

After three months of torment, I saw that gorgeous model from the cider commercials in the middle of Ibn Gvirol Street. I tried talking to her, I tried making her laugh, I ran after her with flowers in my hand, but she didn't give me a second glance. Waiting for her next to the mall was a Mazda sports car with a male model at the wheel, the one from the potato chip commercial. She was about to get into his car and drive off with him. I didn't know what to do, and without even realizing it, I yelled 'Freeze!' She stopped in her tracks. Everyone did. I looked around at all the people frozen there like that, at her, as beautiful as she was in the commercials. I didn't know what to do. On the one hand, I couldn't, I just couldn't let her go. On the other, if she was going to be with me, I wanted it to be because of what I am, because of my inner self, not because I ordered her to. And then it came, the solution. Like an epiphany. I held her hand, looked into her eyes and said, 'Love me for what I am, for what I truly am.' Then I took her back to my apartment and fucked her like a madman. She screamed and dug her nails into my back and said, 'Do it, oh yes, do it to me.' And she loved me, she loved me so much. Just for what I truly am.

ANOTHER OPTION

Suddenly, another option opened up for her. An option that must have always existed, but was, at least as far as she was concerned, inaccessible. She remembered very well how only six months ago, she had looked down from her balcony. And the thing that had paralyzed her neck mumbled through her throat, 'I don't understand how people do that to themselves.' She just didn't understand. But now she does. Not that she has to do it, but the option exists. Like a driver's license, like a visa to the United States. Something she could take advantage of, or not.

There was a time when she wouldn't do that for

guys – 'Suck them off', 'Go down on them', 'Swallow', 'Dive' – it's interesting how all those names they invented for it sound so disgusting. Maybe it was the names that repulsed her. But not any more. Not that she thought it was so great. But she could do it when she thought she should. Another option.

Then they're in bed and she has that 'after' taste in her mouth. Kind of salty-sticky. Something between pretzels and fish. He pulls her on top of him like he always does. Kisses her on the mouth. So he can taste it too. As if to prove that it isn't disgusting. 'What are you thinking about?' he asks. She smiles, thinking about the option. 'Nothing,' she tells him. 'Nothing.'

She wonders if there really is nothing afterwards, or if there is something. Her intuition tells her there's nothing. Because if it's pretty much nothing now, when everything's moving, then it figures that it would be the same afterwards. But not necessarily. There is no 'necessarily'. We have free choice. Nothing or not nothing. All the options are in our hands.

They say she's talented, but what do I know. I roam around her soul, and it's like a deserted apartment. Like a house where the parents have shoved all the furniture into a corner because their son is having a party. With painting, they say, and with texts too. Creative, but quiet and slightly odd.

And I say – go figure her out. Nothing here is clear. Because of her, I feel guilty.

I've always asked myself what girls think when they're doing it. Not the suicide thing, the oral thing. It bothers me. I always used to think that they thought it was to bum them out, humiliate them. I hoped that if I could get inside her head, everything would be different, I'd get some kind of insight. Different my ass, this isn't why I became a writer.

She looks up from the balcony. The sky. Iron bars and the sky. Her thoughts – not sharp at all. The whole thing's kitsch. In the end, she'll die, even though they say she's talented. She'll go down on me and she'll die. She'll die and she'll go down on me. In the name of free choice. In the name of the Movement for the Advancement of Women and Gravitation. And I can tie it all together with a big bang that will play up all my narrative skills. Or not.

WITHOUT HER

What do you do the day the woman of your life dies? I went to Jerusalem and back. There were terrible traffic jams; some film festival was opening. Just getting from downtown to the highway took more than an hour. The guy I was driving with was a young lawyer and an expert in one of those martial arts or something. 'Thank you all,' he mumbled to himself the whole way. 'Thank you to all the people who chose me, and especially to my mother. Without her . . . without her.' He always got stuck like that at 'without her' about three hundred times.

Once we got out of town, and traffic started to flow, he stopped saying thank you and just kept staring at me. 'Are you okay?' he asked every few seconds. 'Are you okay?' and I said yes. 'Are you sure?' he persisted. 'Are you sure?' and I said yes again. I was a little hurt that he'd thanked everyone but me. 'So how about telling me something,' he said. 'Not any of that bullshit you make up, something that really happened to you.' So I told him about the extermination.

My landlord threw in the extermination free of charge. He'd handwritten it in at the bottom of the lease without my even asking for it. A week later, a guy with a plastic jerrycan and a Dr Roach shirt woke me up. He did the whole house in forty minutes and told me to air out the place when I came back that evening and not to wash the floors for a week. As if I would've washed them if he hadn't told me not to.

When I came home after work, there was no floor. Everything was covered with a carpet of legs turned to the ceiling. Three layers of corpses. One or two hundred on each floor tile. Some of them were the size of kittens. One, its belly covered with white spots, was the size of a television. They weren't moving. I asked one of the neighbors for a spade and loaded them into jumbo-size garbage bags. When I'd filled something like fifteen of them, the room started spinning. My head hurt. I went to open all the windows, stepping on crumbling corpses on the way. In the kitchen, I found one swinging from the light fixture. The bug probably realized it was going to die from the poison and decided to hang itself. I loosened the rope and the body fell on me. I almost collapsed; it weighed about seventy kilos. It was wearing a black jacket without pockets, and it didn't have any papers or a watch or anything, not even wings. It reminded me of someone I knew in the army. I felt really sorry for it.

I took the others downstairs in the bags, but I dug that one a grave. And instead of a headstone, I covered it with an empty watermelon carton I'd found near the dumpster. A week later, the exterminator guy came to spray the place again, but I whacked him on the head with a kitchen chair and he was out of there in a flash, didn't even ask why.

When I'd finished telling the story, we were both quiet. Then I asked him if it was true that a lawyer can't inform on his clients, and he said yes. I offered him a cigarette, but he didn't want one. I turned on the radio, but the announcers were on strike. 'Tell me,' he finally asked. 'If it wasn't for the festival, why'd you come to Jerusalem?' 'No reason,' I said. 'A woman I knew died.' 'You knew her for no reason or she died for no reason?' he persisted. Then came the

Shalom intersection, and instead of taking a right, he spun the wheel left straight onto a traffic island.

BUFFALO

I have a friend who's almost a hunter. I mean, he has a hunting rifle and bullets and all, and he spends a lot of time in areas where there are animals, it's just that he doesn't shoot at anything. 'Sometimes,' he tells me, 'I can track a deer or a fox for hours, even days. And when I finally catch up with it, I get close, facing downwind so it won't smell me. I kneel, press my cheek flat against the stock, release the safety catch, get it in my sights and . . . that's it. I don't have to shoot them to know that I can,' he says. 'I just get up and walk away after that. Which, in my opinion, makes it a real sport, not a mere massacre.' He's a weird guy, that friend of mine, I'll be damned if I understand him. His big dream is to go to the States and ambush a herd of buffalo. Just lie calmly at his post with his special bison-hunting rifle, aiming at a single one of that whole sea of animals and tell it, 'You're mine,' then another and another. To just wipe that species off the face of the earth in his head. The reason I'm telling you this is that, yesterday, I went to the basketball stadium with my girlfriend to see a game, and sitting next to me was some unshaven guy who looked like a Palestinian Arab would look if he were born Nordic. He kept looking around at people, muttering. It wasn't till I saw the gun barrel peeking out of his coat pocket that I realized what he was saying. He was just aiming his nine-millimeter at various people, releasing the safety catch and saying quietly to himself, 'You're dead, and so are you.' A few bullets later, when he aimed discreetly at me, I tried to smile calmly and think about my friend with the buffalo. 'You're mine,' he said to himself, leaving me with my crooked grin, and stopped to reload. I stopped too. I took a deep breath, and a strange grunt suddenly came out of my throat. It's just a sport, I said, trying to reassure myself, it doesn't hurt anyone. But in my heart, I knew that if he aimed at my girlfriend too, I'd get up out of my seat in the stands and break all his bones.

PATIENCE

The most patient man in the world was sitting on a bench next to Dizengoff Center. No one was sitting on the bench beside him, not even pigeons. The perverts in the public toilets were making such loud, weird noises that you couldn't ignore them. The most patient man in the world was holding a newspaper in his hand, pretending.

He wasn't really reading, he was waiting for something. No one knew what.

A German tabloid offered ten thousand euros to anyone who found out what the man was waiting for, but no one did. In the exclusive interview he agreed to give to a CNN correspondent, the most patient man in the world said he was waiting for lots of things, but that wasn't the place to list them. 'So where *is* the place?' the persistent journalist asked, but the most patient man in the world didn't answer him, he just waited quietly for the next question. He waited and waited and waited, until finally, they switched the broadcast back to the studio.

People from all over the world made pilgrimages to him to ask what his secret was. Hyperactive brokers, hysterical students, artists desperate for their promised fifteen minutes of fame. The most patient man in the world didn't know exactly what he was supposed to tell them. 'Shave,' he always ended up saying. 'Shave with hot water, it's very soothing.' And all the men would rush right off to their bathrooms and nick their faces in a thousand places. Women said he was a chauvinist. That his macho answer automatically denied every woman her right to attain a state of calm. Women also thought that he was very ugly. Laurie Anderson even wrote a song about him. 'A Very Patient, Ugly Chauvinist Man' was its title. 'His biological clock isn't going anywhere,' is what the chorus said.

The most patient man in the world fell asleep on the bench with his eyes half closed. In his dreams, meteors crashed into the ground with the faint sound of buses, hideous volcanoes erupted with the sound of perverts flushing toilets, and the girl he'd loved for many years told her husband she was leaving him with the cooing of birds. Two meters from him, two pigeons were trying to peck each other's eyes out for no reason. They weren't even fighting about food. 'Shave,' the man told them in his dream. 'Shave with hot water, it's very soothing.'

THE SUMMER OF '76

In the summer of '76, they remodeled our house and added another bathroom. That was my mother's private bathroom, with green tiles, white curtains and a kind of small drawing board she could put on her knees to do crossword puzzles on. The door of this new bathroom had no lock because it was my mother's and no one else was allowed to go inside anyway. We were very happy that summer. My sister, who was best friends with Rina Mor, that year's Miss Universe, married a nice South African dentist who'd immigrated to Israel and they moved to Ra'ananna. My older brother finished the army and got a job as a security guard for Em-Al. My father made a pile on oil-drilling stocks and became a partner in an amusement park. And I always made everyone bring me presents.

'Different people – different dreams –' that's what was written on the American catalog I picked my surprises from. It had everything from a gun that shot potatoes to life-size Spider-Man dolls. And every time my brother flew to America, he let me pick one thing from the catalog. The kids in the neighborhood looked up to me because of my new toys, and they listened to me about everything. On Friday afternoons, my whole class used to go to the park to play baseball with the bat and glove my brother brought me. And I was the biggest champion, because Jeremy, my sister's husband, taught me to throw curve balls that no one could lay a bat on.

Terrible things could happen around me, but they never even touched me. In the Baltic Sea, three sailors ate their captain; the mother of a kid in my school had a boob cut off; Dalit's brother was killed in a training accident in the army. Anat Moser, the prettiest girl in class, said yes, she'd be my girlfriend, and she didn't even talk it over with the other girls. My brother said he was just waiting for my birthday to take me on a trip to America as a gift. Meanwhile, on Saturdays, he'd drive me and Anat to the amusement park in his Swedish car and

I'd tell the park operators that I was Schwartz's son and they'd let us go on all the rides for free.

On holidays, we'd go to visit Grandpa Reuven in Zichron, and when he shook my hand, he'd squeeze it so hard I cried. Then he'd yell at me that I was spoilt and needed to learn to shake hands like a man. He'd always tell my mother she was bringing me up all wrong, that she wasn't preparing me for life. Mom would always apologize and say that actually, she *was* preparing me, it was just that life today wasn't anything like life used to be. That today, you didn't have to know how to make Molotov cocktails from alcohol and nails or how to kill for bread. It was enough to learn how to enjoy life. But Grandpa wouldn't let it go. He'd pinch my ear and whisper that if you want to know how to enjoy life, you also have to know what sadness is. Otherwise, it isn't worth a damn. I tried, but life was so beautiful then, that summer of '76, that no matter how hard I worked at it, I couldn't make myself sad about anything.